RANGE GRAB

Range Grab

CORBA SUNMAN

A Black Horse Western

ROBERT HALE · LONDON

© Corba Sunman 1996
First published in Great Britain 1996

ISBN 0 7090 5746 6

Robert Hale Limited
Clerkenwell House
Clerkenwell Green
London EC1R 0HT

Photoset in North Wales by
Derek Doyle & Associates, Mold, Clwyd.
Printed in Great Britain by
St Edmundsbury Press Ltd, Bury St Edmunds, Suffolk.
Bound by WBC Book Manufacturers Limited,
Bridgend, Mid-Glamorgan.

ONE

The setting sun was taking a last red-eyed squint at the Texas range when Brad Devlone began to look for a camp-site. He had ridden across the heat-tortured prairie for more hours than he cared to recall, bone-weary from the jolting saddle and parched by the vein-drying sunlight of the long day.

'It's time we found a spot to light and rest,' he observed, speaking to his horse, and the bay stallion's ears twitched as it shook its head at the unaccustomed sound, for all day there had been nothing but the thud of hooves, the creaking of saddle leather and the stertorous breathing of the animal itself. 'I figure it's still twenty miles to Ash Bend, so we'll bed down rough tonight and make up for it in town tomorrow.'

The bay nodded as if in agreement as Devlone's narrowed blue eyes noted the dense shadows growing around him. He was a big man, raw-boned and heavy-muscled; in his prime at thirty-one, for the toughness of his way of life had honed him to peak fitness. He was wearing dusty range clothes topped by a high-crowned black Stetson which was decorated with a leather band studded with metal conchos. His red shirt was streaked with dust, his leather vest open and flapping in the hot breeze. His legs were encased in shot-gun chaps, his feet enclosed by high-heeled riding boots. A .45 Peacemaker Colt was buckled around his waist, which was complemented by a Winchester 30-30 nestling in a saddle boot under his right thigh.

The bay topped a ridge, and Devlone reined up when he saw yellow light spilling from several windows in the middle distance. A cattle ranch! Relief filled him, and he shrugged his shoulders, touching spurs to the bay.

'We may be lucky after all,' he mused. 'Get on there!'

The bay went forward obediently, presently finding a narrow trail which led into the yard of the cow spread before them. Devlone reined up at the gate and glanced at the big sign supported on posts above the gate. *Nathan Palmer*, he read, squinting his eyes in the shadows. *Broken P Ranch. Keep Out. This means you*.

'Nathan Palmer ain't a hospitable man, it seems like!' Devlone leaned down to open the gate. He gigged the bay through, and, as he paused to close the gate, a bullet whined past his head. He froze as the ensuing report sent a string of echoes through the gathering night.

A rider emerged from the cover of a nearby draw and approached with a sixgun steady in his right hand.

'Whatsa matter with you?' The guard was big and tough. 'Don't you read good? Nat Palmer went to a lot of trouble to get that sign painted, and he sure as hell don't want saddle bums riding in as if it wasn't there.'

'I got business with Palmer.' Devlone eased himself in the saddle, and the bay took several dancing steps towards the guard.

'Nobody's got any business this side of the gate unless Palmer asks him in,' came the terse reply. 'You got an invite, mister?'

'I told you I got business here,' Devlone replied.

'A hardcase, huh?' The man cocked his gun, the trio of clicks sounding ominous in the tense silence.

'You got orders to shoot visitors in cold blood?'

'I don't scare you none, huh?' The man waggled the gun. 'Supposin' I tell you I got orders to shoot on sight?'

'I'd say you was running a bluff.' Devlone shrugged. 'Your warning shot would have been through me, not over my head.'

'So you're wearing smart-pants!' The guard shook his head. 'I guess I'll take you up to the house. The boss can make up his own mind about you. Git going! Follow the trail. And don't forget I'll be right behind you, itching to perforate your spine some!'

Devlone kneed his horse forward and passed the man, ignoring the threat of the levelled gun, his mind busy on what he had been told two weeks before at Ranger Headquarters in Houston, about the folk inhabiting this part of the range in northern Texas. There was bad trouble in Simpson County, with signs that human greed was behind it, and that was why he was here, trouble-hunting! A stranger coming into the county to stand up for law and order because local lawmen could not cope.

Full darkness was falling as he neared the front of the sprawling ranch house, and a low voice called urgently from the dense shadows around it.

'Hold up there and declare yourself!' came the challenge.

'It's me, boss,' replied Devlone's escort. 'This stranger came in through the gate like it wasn't there, so either he cain't read or he's dumb.'

Devlone smiled as he kneed his horse to the hitchrail before the porch, his eyes straining to pick up details of the tall figure standing there.

'Who are you, mister, and what do you want?' demanded the rancher.

'Are you Nathan Palmer?'

'You got me to rights. What's your business?'

'I'm Brad Devlone. Frank Wade asked me to drop in on you if I was ever out this way.'

'Frank Wade, huh! Hell, I ain't set eyes on Big Frank in a coon's age! How is that long, curly wolf these days?'

'Beginning to show his years! But he said you'd make me welcome, so here I am!'

'Get down and come in, Devlone. Any man recommended by Frank Wade is welcome here. Rafe, take care of his horse!'

Devlone dismounted, trailed his reins and ascended three steps to the porch. The tall figure of the rancher turned to enter the house and Devlone followed closely, looking around with interest as yellow lamplight enveloped him. Palmer turned to face him, his narrowed brown eyes taking in the essential details of this tough-looking newcomer.

'Around here a man would be a fool to accept a stranger at face value,' observed Palmer. He was tall and thin, his face burned almost black by many years under the pitiless sun, and he looked older than his fifty-four years. 'You got something on you proving Big Frank sent you?'

Devlone stuck his left forefinger and thumb inside his cartridge belt and produced his Ranger badge, a silver star set in a silver circle which lay in his big palm, glinting in the lamplight.

'This should be good enough for you.' He returned the badge to its hidden pocket. 'Such is the nature of the reports received about the trouble here I've been told to handle this chore under cover.'

'I wrote Big Frank about the trouble.' Palmer took a bottle of whiskey and two glasses from a nearby tray. 'Sit down while we talk, Devlone.'

'I'd rather eat than drink whiskey at this time,' countered Devlone. 'I've been in the saddle since sun-up today, the same as every day for the past week, being in a hurry to get here.' He sat down in an easy chair and relaxed. 'I didn't allow much time for eating and the like!'

Palmer nodded. 'The cook'll sling a meal together for you.' He moved to an inner door. 'I'm sure glad you've showed up at last. I've been looking for someone for the past week. Give me a minute and I'll get Cookie to rustle you up some grub.'

Devlone relaxed in his seat. His gaze took in his surroundings, missing nothing. The big room was well furnished, comfortable, but lacked the softer touch of a woman's hand. He recalled Captain Wade's words about Nat Palmer. 'Brad, you can trust your life with Palmer. He's white clear through!' Devlone shook his head. His life was on the line all right, as always, but he did not anticipate much trouble. A stranger, coming in for a fresh viewpoint, could usually spot the troublemakers quickly, and the local law would back his play once he learned the identity of the badmen.

Palmer reappeared in the doorway, nodding. 'Grub won't be long. I reckon you stayed last night in San Tomas.'

'Yeah.' Devlone's blue eyes narrowed as he recalled the previous night. 'I was ambushed there by two men, and several times today I saw their tracks coming this way ahead of me. I figure those back-shooters are itching for another chance to put me under.

'Hell, that's bad!' Palmer's taut features showed concern. 'I never let on to anyone that I'd contacted the Rangers!'

Devlone shrugged. 'It ain't the first time I been

shot at. And now I'm here, what can you tell me? As a local man, you should have a good idea who's breaking the law in this neck of the woods.'

'That's the trouble!' Palmer frowned. 'Whoever's behind this crookedness has sure got more than his share of savvy! The blame seems to fall first in one place, then another.'

'So there's a deep-dug crook running things, huh?' Devlone nodded. 'Who do you figure is behind it?'

Palmer shook his head. 'I'm afraid to point the finger in case I pick the wrong man! I've had cause to suspect just about everyone in the county. It's like trying to rope a cloud, Devlone! It just ain't possible!'

'Do you have a map of the county?'

'Sure! In my office. Come and take a look.'

'Thanks. I'd like to get the local layout fixed in my mind.'

They went into Palmer's office, where a large-scale map was pinned to a wall. Devlone studied it while Palmer pointed out the various ranches surrounding his own spread and the position of Ash Bend, eight miles to the east.

'There you have it,' said Palmer. 'North is Joe Wyatt's JW spread. He also owns a big half of Ash Bend. To the west is Teasdale's Tall T, and south are a lot of small spreads. I tell you, Devlone, I've racked my brains about this trouble till I thought I was going crazy, and I still ain't none the wiser. All I do know is that men are being killed, stock stolen, and money is draining away from this range faster than water can run out of a hole in a bucket.'

'You paint a bad picture!' Devlone thrust out his bottom lip. 'But I'll start making enquiries.' He paused, eyes narrowing as he considered. 'If I need gun help any time, can I count on you and your outfit?'

'You bet!' Palmer blinked. 'Just send word and we'll come running!' He turned as an old man appeared in the doorway.

'That grub you asked for is ready,' said the newcomer, his eyes narrowing when he saw Devlone. 'I put it on the table back there.'

'Thanks, Cookie. It's for this young feller.'

The old cook turned away and they returned to the big room where a large plate of food was waiting. Devlone needed no second invitation to eat, tucking in while listening to Palmer's low voice providing information on the local situation. By the time his hunger was appeased he had a good idea of the prominent men in Simpson County and the salient points of the trouble.

'When are you going into town?' Palmer poured Devlone a whiskey.

'I'd continue now but my horse is played out so I'd better rest up until the morning. I guess another day won't hurt, huh?'

'That's sensible.' Palmer half turned his head, listening intently, and Devlone stiffened when he caught the sound of rapidly approaching hooves out there in the night. 'What's going on?' Palmer frowned. 'Nobody rides that fast in the dark unless it's life or death!'

Devlone opened his mouth to answer, but gunfire crashed, blasting out the silence, and glass flew from shattered windows as bullets splintered into the front wall of the house. Palmer uttered a yell and hurled himself sideways. Devlone dropped flat to the floor, listening to hammering guns and the angry thud of bullets crackling through sun-warped woodwork....

The shooting cut out almost instantly, and receding hooves echoed sharply amidst the fading echoes. Devlone got to his feet and crossed to the nearest window, canting his head to catch the last of the receding hoofbeats.

'Boss!' Devlone recognized the guard's voice, just outside the window. 'Are you OK in there?'

'Yeah!' Palmer's tall figure moved into the doorway and became silhouetted against the night sky. 'I reckon that was done to scare us. But it ain't gonna work, no siree! Did you see who they were, Rafe?'

'Nope, boss. They was in here so sudden. But I figger there was four of them. They sure threw handfuls of lead at the house.'

'They couldn't miss with all the lights shining,' growled Palmer. 'Stay out of the yard, Rafe, or you'll muss up their tracks. In the morning we might be able to pick up something!'

'I wouldn't count on that was I in your boots.' The guard laughed cynically. 'But I tell you something, boss, those riders came whoopin' and hollerin' like redskins, and I reckon one of 'em sounded mighty like Billy Teasdale. You know that kind of high-pitched laugh he's got! You couldn't mistake that in a million! Well, I figure I heard him in that bunch!'

'That don't make sense.' Palmer cursed. 'We ain't got nothing going with the Tall T! Hell, me and Teasdale have agreed to help each other out.'

'I'll ride on,' cut in Devlone. 'With someone to point out the Tall T.'

'You sure ain't gonna let the grass grow under your feet!' Palmer nodded. 'I'll ride with you if you can stand my company. Rafe, saddle up our horses!'

'I don't want you to ride into the Tall T with me,' Devlone said. 'I prefer to work alone. But the sooner I get started the better.'

Minutes later they were crossing the range in near darkness, and, as the rancher chatted, Devlone picked up further snippets of local information that might be useful later. Eventually, Palmer topped a rise and reined in.

'I'll stop here,' he said. 'Follow the trail into the valley and you'll find the Tall T.'

'Thanks for your help,' Devlone replied. 'I'll be out to see you again, so don't do anything until I make contact.'

'Sure thing!' Palmer turned his horse back the way they had come. 'I hope you can light a fire under those crooks!' he called over his shoulder.

Devlone lifted a hand in acknowledgement and continued. Alone again, he settled in his saddle. This surely was troubled range, and a man could not afford to take chances. He set the bay into a lope and followed the trail into a narrow valley. There were no lights anywhere, and he wondered about that as he approached Teasdale's cow spread....

Riding into the yard, Devlone peered around. A barn was to the left, with a low building still farther left, which he took to be a bunkhouse. The sound of his hooves echoed in the shadows, but as he reined in preparatory to calling the house his ears picked up a distant drumming sound, which he recognized instantly as the hoofbeats of several horses rapidly approaching.

He twisted in the saddle, the fingers of his right hand reaching to the butt of his holstered Colt. But the night was too dark to permit sharp vision, with nothing more than starshine softening the contours of his surroundings. Yet his keen eyes caught the grim sight of concerted movement coming from his left, and he guessed a raid was developing. Swinging out of his saddle, his movement coincided with a gun being fired from the dense shadows of the ranch house, and he heard the angry whine of a bullet closely passing his right ear. Ducking away, he dragged his Winchester from its saddle boot and dived clear of the plunging horse, which ran away to the rear of the house.

Devlone hit the dust beside the well and peered at the approaching riders, mindful of the fact that someone in the house had tried to shoot him. The next instant gunfire crackled echoingly, and red and orange muzzle-flashes split the close night as six riders came hammering into the dusty yard.

Lifting his Winchester, Devlone swung the barrel and squinted through the sights. The riders came on, while three guns quickly returned fire from the ranch buildings. Devlone fired, and as gunsmoke blew back into his face he saw his man pitch sideways out of the saddle, an echoing cry shrilling through the heavier blasts of shooting.

Bullets raked the front of the house as the riders galloped through the yard, heading for the rear of the ranch, and Devlone swung his rifle, covering their progress. He fired again when his sights lined up on a fleeing figure, and a second rider spilled out of leather to hit the hard ground with a thump. Then the riders were gone around the corner of the ranch house and the shooting cut off as if a thick curtain had fallen over the cow spread.

Devlone was breathing heavily as he arose, rifle ready. The sound of hooves was receding, and he knew the attack had been hit and run. He got to his feet warily, eyes slitted against the gloom. A voice was calling from the bunkhouse in a high-pitched tone, demanding to know what was going on, and a tough voice replied from the house, warning everyone to stay under cover.

'Hank,' reported the voice from the bunkhouse. 'There's someone hunkered down by the well. He was shooting at the raiders, and nailed two of them. Can you see him?'

'I fired a warning shot at someone just before

the raiders struck,' came the harsh reply. 'Hey, you out there by the well! Declare yourself.'

'I'm Brad Devlone. I was riding in when those men hit the place. Bring a lantern and we'll take a look at those who are down.'

'Thanks for buying into this on my side,' came the reply. 'Keep your eyes lifting and I'll come out with a light.'

'Pa, don't do it!' a woman's voice called shrilly, and it was laced with a mixture of shock and fear. 'It could be a trick to lure you into the open.'

'You stay put, Rana, while I go out there,' the rough voice retorted.

Devlone turned as a figure emerged from the house carrying a lantern, and he watched the shadows as the man came across the yard. Narrowing his eyes against the yellow light, he reached a fallen rider at about the same time the man with the lantern arrived, and they stood together looking down at the inert figure. There was blood on the man's shirt front and at one corner of his mouth. His eyes were wide and staring, as if he had caught a glimpse of hell in his last moment of life.

'Any idea who he is?' Devlone glanced at his companion, who was tall and lean, with fair hair that was long and lank at the back of his neck.

'I ain't never seen him before,' replied the man. 'So what the hell is going on? I've never knowed so many strangers to be on this range.'

'Someone is importing hardcases,' Devlone said. 'Who are you, friend?'

'Hank Teasdale. This is my spread, the Tall T. And I'm mighty pleased to see you! You sure showed up at the right moment! Most of my crew are in town tonight, and there's only me, the cook and my daughter to watch over the place.'

'I'm passing through,' said Devlone, 'and stopped by to ask the way to the nearest town.'

'You're welcome to stay till sun-up,' offered Teasdale. 'You'd be a mighty comforting *hombre* to have around.'

'Let's take a look at the other one I hit,' Devlone countered, and, when they had walked across the yard to where the second man lay, he dropped to one knee beside the figure and examined it while Teasdale held the lantern high over them. 'He's dead too!' There was no satisfaction in Devlone. 'I tried to wing them but the light was bad! Any idea who he is?'

'I got no ideas about anything any more!' Teasdale cursed softly. 'This is another face I never set eyes on until now. Someone's sure playing a deep game, and I hope I got a gun in my hand when he's unmasked. Folks have been murdered and robbed, and now ranches are being shot up. No one is safe, and I figure the time has come for honest men to take the law into their own hands.'

'That ain't a good idea even if you know who the guilty men are,' said Devlone. 'I figure you should leave law dealing to lawmen.'

'Mister, you don't know our local lawmen!' Teasdale laughed cynically. 'But when you do

meet them you'll understand why I'm talking like
I do. Any resemblance between them and good
lawmen sure is accidental!'

'I guess I'll be meeting them pretty quick.'
Devlone shrugged. 'We'll have to tote these bodies
into town and report the incident.'

'Come into the house first and let's have us a
drink. I could sure use one!' Teasdale glanced
around. 'Then we'll ride into town together. You'll
need my word to back up your story of what
happened.'

Devlone shook his head as they turned to walk
to the house. Teasdale's story of local events was
commonplace, times being what they were. There
certainly was bad trouble riding this range and
his arrival was none too soon. It was the old story
of greedy men out to make a profit and not caring
who was killed in the process! But the honest men
of the county were not prepared to be ridden over
roughshod, which was to the good! All they needed
was to be organized, and that, Devlone told
himself, was where he came in!

TWO

They were a silent cavalcade on the ride to Ash Bend. Devlone rode beside Rana Teasdale, who said nothing during the eight-mile trip, while Hank Teasdale and Zach Carter followed them, each leading a saddle horse carrying the draped figure of a dead man. The thudding of hooves and creaking leather filled their ears, and Devlone had to fight against tiredness as he eased himself in the jolting saddle, his mind struggling to get to grips with what had occurred since his arrival on this range. But this was a new case, and as yet there were no positive leads to aid him in his search for the troublemakers.

When lights showed in the middle distance Rana Teasdale stirred in her saddle and glanced at Devlone, who caught her movement and transferred his attention to her.

'You're a fool,' she observed in a low voice. 'Riding into town like this can only end in disaster! The law in this county operates for the big men, and the men you killed were working for them, so what do you hope to prove? They'll frame you with murder despite your witnesses, and my father is just as big a fool as you for thinking he can use this incident to open up the trouble we've got. All he'll do is line himself up against the big men, and they'll trample him underfoot the minute they get wind of what's going on!'

Hank Teasdale drew level. 'That's Ash Bend ahead, Devlone,' he commented. 'Watch your step around here. The local law is mighty tough on strangers who butt into trouble which ain't theirs! Tom Ballew is the county sheriff, but he's only a mouthpiece for Weasel Joe Wyatt, who owns most of the business in town and out here on the range. He's got all the earmarks of a land shark, or I don't know the difference between a twelve-dollar bugle and my butt!'

'I get the picture,' Devlone nodded soberly. 'So that's the way the wind blows, huh?'

They rode down a decline, and Devlone began to figure the town was much farther away than it looked. But eventually they drew close enough to see the outlines of low buildings. Hank Teasdale led the way into a wide, rutted street, and Devlone narrowed his eyes as he looked along its gloomy length where lamps gleamed here and there at various windows. Teasdale seemed to be making for a spot where two lamps shone close together, and, as they drew nearer, Devlone saw a large board fixed to a wooden awning out front which bore the legend SHERIFF'S OFFICE & JAIL.

They reined up at the hitching-rail and Devlone stepped down from his saddle and stretched. He

wrapped his reins around the pole and glanced
into the surrounding shadows. There was a saloon
across the way, judging by the sounds emanating
from a brightly lit building, and he moistened his
lips, for it had been a long, hot day. But he kept
his mind on the grim business to hand and waited
for Teasdale to lead the way into the law office.

'Rana, get yourself a room at the hotel and stay
put till I come for you,' Teasdale told his daughter,
and his tone was ragged, as if he were labouring
under some suddenly incurred pressure. 'Leave
your hoss and I'll take care of it. Zach, go along
with Rana and make sure she puts up safely, then
come back here. You'll likely have to make a
statement about what happened at the ranch, and
I want you to back any kind of play we have to
make.'

'Sure, boss!' The Tall T cook swung his mount
obediently.

'We'll see Sheriff Ballew now!' Teasdale glanced
at Devlone as he stepped on to the boardwalk, the
sound of his boots echoing in the dusty shadows.
He reached the door of the office and pushed it
open to enter like a man who was playing out a
hand he did not really like.

Devlone pushed forward quickly, and was at
Teasdale's elbow when they crossed the threshold
of the law office, his narrowed eyes noting the
interior at a glance. There was not much to look
at. A battered desk stood in the near left-hand
corner. There was a rifle rack on the back wall
containing five long guns of various calibres and

types, and a row of posters gave the hard features and details of half a dozen wanted men.

Two men were seated at the desk, playing cards and smoking long cheroots that emitted curling wisps of acrid blue smoke. The remains of two suppers littered a corner of the desk, and a big bunch of keys lay glinting in the strong lamplight. Sheriff Tom Ballew, pushing forty-five, was seated behind the desk. He was paunchy, his seamed face bloated and pale in an unhealthy way. His black Stetson was pushed back from his rugged forehead, revealing long, greasy hair, and his hard brown eyes narrowed when they focused on the two newcomers. He rolled a cheroot from one corner of his slit-like mouth to the other, then spoke around it.

'What you doing in town, Teasdale? Still looking for trouble?'

The other man, wearing a town marshal's badge, sniggered as he shifted in his chair to look at the doorway. He was thin, with a long, bony frame and blue eyes glinting with a fervent light. His movements were quick, almost nervous, except, Devlone figured, that he probably didn't have a nerve in his whole body. He looked dangerous, like a coiled snake ready to strike.

'I brung a load of trouble, Denning,' asserted Teasdale. 'We packed in two dead men.' He launched into an account of what had happened, and Devlone watched the lawmen for reaction as the story unfolded, noting the way he was eyed as his part in the events was described.

Sheriff Ballew cursed and pushed himself to his feet. He was wearing a Colt .45 holstered low down on his right hip, and his right hand dropped to the butt as he studied Devlone.

'Can you put names to the dead men?' he demanded.

'Never seen them before!' Teasdale shook his head. 'I been telling you about night riders for a long time, Ballew, but you never believed me. Now you got proof, and it's come the hard way.'

'And this feller nailed them, huh?' The sheriff came round the desk to confront Devlone, his pasty face aggressive. 'Who are you, mister?'

'The name is Devlone. I happened to reach the Tall T yard a jump ahead of a bunch of riders who came out of the night shooting and yelling. When I nearly caught a slug I started shooting back.' Devlone shrugged. 'Too bad for them I usually hit what I aim at, come sunlight or starshine.'

Marshal Denning got to his feet, his pale eyes glinting. Ash dropped from his cheroot, and there was a brown stain on his taut lips. His narrowed eyes were veiled, filled with the brightness of a predator scenting a victim.

'I'll take a look at the stiffs,' he said. He was taller than average, and was wearing a dark store suit with a broad leather gunbelt buckled around his waist. His boots made no noise on the boards as he walked to the door.

Devlone kept his attention on the sheriff, who was watching him, and the man's expression warned him to be on his guard.

'Devlone, I run a clean county here,' Ballew blustered, 'and I don't like strangers coming in and stirring up trouble.'

'Nobody likes a troublemaker,' Devlone agreed, moving slightly to bring the street door into his field of vision. He heard the town marshal's boots on the sidewalk, and the man re-entered the office, shaking his head.

'I never seen either of them two before, Sheriff,' he said. 'They look like a couple of hardcases, probably on the run from the law.'

'So that's how you're gonna explain what happened!' Teasdale's eyes were glinting with anger. 'Sheriff, there's been too much covered up on this range lately, and it's about time you did something about this lawlessness.'

'You leave me to tend law business!' Ballew snarled. 'Sit down and tell me again what happened. I need reports before I can start looking into it.'

'What is there to tell?' Teasdale was becoming impatient. 'A bunch of riders hit my place ashooting like all come-out, and two of 'em were knocked out of their saddles! That's it, and by grab it's about time we started fighting back! Devlone, if you need a riding job then you got one with my outfit. You only got to say. You're the kind of man I need to have around. With your gun skill I can hold my own against whoever is out to hog-tie this range, and the sooner we start fighting back the better I'll like it!'

'I don't agree with ranchers hiring gunslicks,'

growled Ballew. 'Devlone, you shake the dust of this range off your boots tomorrow at dawn.'

The street door clattered open and a man wearing a deputy's star entered. He was tall, thickset, with a swagger in his walk and a mean expression on his heavy face. He paused in midstride and froze when his narrowed gaze fell upon Devlone, who immediately recalled the night he spent in San Tomas when two men ambushed him, for he had glimpsed their shadowed faces in the flaring light of gunflashes, and figured one of the murderous pair was before him.

'Hey, there are two stiffs roped to saddles out there!' the deputy said.

'We know, Snark!' Ballew shook his head. 'Did you take a look at 'em?'

'Nope.' The deputy frowned.

'Then go and do it and see if you can put a name to either of them.' Ballew's dark eyes glittered. 'Where in hell have you been? I sent you to San Tomas to handle a simple chore and you been gone three days!'

'It wasn't so simple, Sheriff!' The deputy went out again while Devlone considered his suspicions. So the deputy had been in San Tomas recently! He waited until Snark returned, shaking his head. 'I never set eyes on either of them fellers before,' he stated flatly. 'What happened?'

'They were shot out at Teasdale's spread.' The sheriff moved back around the desk and sat down.

'There'll be an inquest tomorrow morning, and everyone concerned better be there. And you quit this range soon as the inquest is over, Devlone.'

Before Devlone could reply the street door was thrust open and two men filled the doorway. Devlone recognized one as Nathan Palmer, the Broken P rancher, and stepped back a pace as the office seemed to overfill. Palmer slammed the door violently, and Ballew sprang up from his seat.

'What in hell are you trying to do, knock the door off its hinges?' he yelled.

'Mebbe I'm hoping to wake up this law department,' replied Palmer. 'I was visited earlier this evening by a bunch of hardcases who shot up my place on their way through.'

'You, too!' Ballew sighed. 'What in Hades is going on around here?'

Palmer looked frowningly at Teasdale. 'By the look on your face, Hank, you've had trouble too!' he observed.

Teasdale explained, and Palmer glanced at Devlone.

'Two of 'em were shot out of their saddles by Devlone here,' Teasdale concluded. 'But nobody knows who they are. I'm hoping someone in town can recognize 'em.'

Palmer met Devlone's impassive gaze, his eyes gleaming.

'I saw those two stiffs outside,' he said. 'They're strangers to me. But this is a step in the right direction! If that crew was hit every time they tried something they wouldn't be so keen to ride roughshod over the range.'

'I'm against folks taking the law into their own hands,' protested Ballew. 'If it goes on then someone will have a murder charge brung against them.'

'Does the law say a man can't protect his property?' demanded Teasdale. 'Until we can find out who's behind this trouble we have to shoot on sight.'

'Maybe we do have something to work on!' Palmer's tone hardened. 'Your son Billy, Hank. Where's he at right now?'

'Billy?' Teasdale's expression tightened. 'What about him?'

'He's got a distinctive laugh, and it was heard in my yard tonight when the hardcases rode through!'

'Do you figure Billy was one of that bunch?' Teasdale's face filled with disbelief. 'Heck, they rode through my yard shooting hell out of the place! You reckon Billy is mixed up in that?'

'I ain't making accusations,' responded Palmer. 'But I'd sure like to hear Billy's account of his movements this evening.'

'He's in town!' Teasdale turned to the door. 'Let's go look him up together. You ain't the only one wanting to know what he was doing.'

'Just hold your hosses!' Ballew shouted. 'If there's any questions to be asked, I'll do it. I've warned you about taking the law into your own hands so clear out and leave me to do my job. Devlone, get out of town after the inquest tomorrow or you'll see the inside of this jail.'

Teasdale and Palmer turned to leave, their faces grim, and Devlone knew they would not obey the sheriff's orders. As he turned to follow them he heard Ballew speak to Snark.

'Snark, what in hell happened in San Tomas? Did you find that guy?'

'I'll tell you about it, Sheriff,' the deputy responded, throwing a glance at Devlone, who met his gaze obliquely.

Devlone continued out to the sidewalk, certain now that his suspicions of Snark were well founded. He paused to look around the street. Teasdale and Palmer were already walking towards the saloon, and Devlone looked at the two dead men sprawled across their saddles. There was another horse tethered to the hitchrail which had not been there when they rode up.

Figuring it was Snark's horse, he lifted its right foreleg and ran his fingers around the shoe to discover a narrow gap in the outer edge, where a piece of metal was missing. He nodded, having noted the peculiar print of that shoe several times on his ride from San Tomas, aware that one of the ambushers had ridden the horse that made it! He set out to follow the ranchers, convinced that Snark had been one of the two men who ambushed him in San Tomas. He determined to check up on Snark later. But right now he wanted to hear Billy Teasdale's account of his recent movements.

The saloon was a large wooden building, brightly lit and noisy. Music was spilling from

inside as Devlone stepped on to the boardwalk,
and there was the hum of many voices. A sign over
the batwings announced the proprietor's name,
Joe Wyatt, and Devlone recalled that Teasdale
had used the nickname 'Weasel Joe' when
mentioning Wyatt. He shouldered through the
batwings and paused on the threshold of the large
room. There was a long bar on the right stretching
the whole length of the room, and four tenders
were busy serving the men bellied up to it. Games
of chance were dotted around the room, and there
were small tables and chairs where men sat and
drank or played cards.

Teasdale made his way to the left, where six
men were playing cards at a corner table, and
Palmer followed resolutely. Devlone paused to
look around, his gaze immediately alighting on a
massively framed man standing halfway along
the bar. That had to be Weasel Joe Wyatt, he
figured, for he had been given Wyatt's description
back at Ranger Headquarters with the warning
that the businessman was making big tracks in
Simpson County. Wyatt was dressed in a dark
store suit and a fancy shirt, with a red flower in
his buttonhole and a glittering stickpin in his tie.
Devlone estimated that the man was at least
six-three in height and weighed two hundred and
fifty pounds, which, apart from a wide, protruding
belly, seemed to be all fighting weight. A large
cigar protruded from Wyatt's thick lips, and the
saloonman was talking around it to an intently
listening gunman standing at his shoulder.

The gunman was worthy of a second look, and Devlone took in the twin pearl-handled Colts holstered low on the man's hips on crossed cartridge belts. Dressed in unrelieved black and wearing a black Stetson, the gunnie's appearance was strikingly ominous, and Devlone frowned when recognition came to him. Trig Colton! Devlone let his gaze rove, noting that there were far more gunmen and hardcases present than normally showed in a peaceful community, and their presence said much for the local situation, for such men were attracted to trouble like buzzards to dead meat.

Devlone turned his attention to Teasdale and Palmer, who had reached the corner table where the players had stopped their game to look up. One of them was on his feet, red-faced and angry. It had to be Billy Teasdale, decided Devlone, for there was a family resemblance to the Tall T rancher, and the youngster was not happy at being accosted by his father. Devlone started across to the corner, aware that three cowboys were converging on the table, and Joe Wyatt was taking an interest in the proceedings. Devlone saw him nudge Trig Colton and jerk a thumb in the direction of the corner.

Slowing, Devlone looked around and saw other gunmen watching the corner. Tension was filtering into the atmosphere. The piano player faltered in his rhythm, picked up again, and continued in a stilted fashion. Devlone wondered what had happened in the county before his arrival, for an explosive situation now existed, and to his trained eye it was obvious that a mere spark could ignite it with tragic results.

'I asked you a question, Billy,' Hank Teasdale rapped, 'and I want a straight answer or there'll be hell to pay!'

'What's goin' on, Pa? You tryin' to embarrass me in front of my friends? I'm old enough to tend my own business!'

'Don't get smart with me, boy! There's been some trouble and I heard you were mixed up in it.'

'That's a damn lie!' Billy Teasdale stiffened. 'Who told you that?'

'Blustering like a horned toad don't clear you, son!' Palmer spoke in a cold, angry tone. 'You got a laugh in a thousand, and it was heard tonight when a bunch of hardcases rode through my yard, hollerin' and shootin'! So don't bother to deny it.'

A buzz ran through the big room, and Devlone, watching points, saw Weasel Joe Wyatt trade glances with Trig Colton. Then the big saloonman pushed his massive bulk from the bar and came to the corner like a runaway train, pushing men aside and thrusting chairs out of his path. He reached Hank Teasdale's side and halted, standing head and shoulders over the tall rancher.

'What's going on here?' His powerful voice originated from deep inside his barrel-like chest. 'You're like to cause a disturbance, Teasdale, and interrupt the pleasure of my patrons.'

'We can go outside and settle this,' said Palmer, ignoring Wyatt.

Devlone glanced around and saw Denning, the town marshal, push through the batwings, and sight of the lawman sent a pang through Devlone's chest for his instincts were warning that much was wrong in this set-up.

'You said something about a raid on your place tonight, Palmer,' intoned Wyatt, and Devlone heard the breath rasping in the big man's chest. 'What time did it happen? And I better tell you before you start implicating Billy Teasdale that he's been sitting here since five this afternoon.'

'That's right, Pa!' Billy gazed defiantly at his father, his pale eyes filled with anger and frustration. 'You know what time I left the ranch. I came straight to town and walked in here for a game of poker. I ain't left the place since. So how come you're so all-fired eager to believe the worst about me, huh?'

'I ain't happy about this,' said Palmer, glancing at Devlone, who shrugged, intimating by expression and manner that on the evidence presented there was nothing he could do about this particular situation, although he sensed that Wyatt was covering up for Billy Teasdale. Palmer grimaced and turned his back on the corner, disgust showing plainly on his weathered face. 'I guess we ain't gonna get anywhere with this line,' he grated. 'So in future my crew will shoot to kill any time they find strangers on my range.'

'And that goes for me, too!' added Hank Teasdale. 'It's time we called a halt to this. We got to stand together or we'll be picked off piecemeal until there's no one left to fight.'

'We'll do it,' promised Palmer. 'I'll call a special meeting of the Cattleman's Association to bring all the ranchers in behind us. After tonight we stick together!'

Devlone realized the heat had gone out of the situation and turned aside to the bar. His throat was parched, and he had a stack of impressions to file away for later consideration. He bought a beer and was drinking it when the town marshal appeared at his elbow.

'Devlone, how'd you get mixed up in this?' he asked. 'You sure as hell are making a noose for your neck! Was I in your boots I'd be long gone now.'

'You heard the sheriff say I got to stick around for the inquest!' Devlone set down his beer and wiped his mouth on a dusty sleeve.

'Yeah! Well you don't know what that inquest might decide!' Denning grinned. 'Was I in your boots, I'd hightail it out of here.'

'That could look like an admission of guilt,' replied Devlone, smiling. 'I ain't about to act so foolish, Marshal!'

'So you'd rather run the risk of getting a rope put around your neck, huh? Well, it's no skin off my nose, mister, and it'll be your funeral!'

Devlone gazed after Denning as the man moved away, aware that the marshal was not the type to warn a stranger out of the goodness of his heart. So they wanted him to run for another reason! He nodded, his mind thrusting up reasons why that should be. A local deputy had ambushed him the night before in San Tomas, and the sheriff implicated himself by enquiring if the deputy had found the man he had been sent to get!

Further, Snark had frozen on spotting Devlone, his guilty reaction setting the seal on Devlone's reasoning. So he had to learn what he could from Snark. He finished his beer and turned to the door, his quick glance noting the positions of Wyatt and Chick Denning. His eyes narrowed slightly when he saw the two standing just along the bar, talking animatedly, and now there was no sign of Trig Colton!

Devlone knew he could not afford to let the grass grow under his feet. It was obvious that Snark had ambushed him because the local law had got word of a Texas Ranger coming into the county. Ranger Headquarters usually notified the county law of such an event, so Ballew would have had a description of him! Devlone knew he could expect no mercy from the killers. So he had to strike first, and hard. He went out into the night, instinctively flattening himself against the front wall of the saloon while he checked the surrounding shadows. He had already been shot at from cover and knew what to expect. This was a deep game! Someone was playing for high stakes. Men had been killed, and there would be no end to the violence until those responsible had been dealt with.

He crossed the street to collect his horse from the hitchrail in front of the law office, and the moment he was in the open he sensed that he had made a mistake. An alarm flashed through him and he reacted instinctively, throwing himself flat in the dust, and at that moment gunfire split the night and he heard hot lead crackling around him in the uncertain darkness....

THREE

Devlone hit the ground and rolled as bullets cut
through the space his body had occupied scant
seconds before. He heard slugs thudding into the
surrounding dust and kept moving, pausing only
to snake his Colt .45 out of its greased holster. His
narrowed gaze picked out two sources of gunfire,
and he saw that his ambushers had got him
between them. Flaring reddish flashes were
illuminating the mouth of an alley opposite while
the second gun was throwing lead at him from the
dark doorway of a store to the right. Booming
echoes rolled across the town, and, in the
background, dogs were barking furiously, aroused
by the raucous disturbance.

Levelling his sixgun, Devlone returned fire
without conscious thought, bracketing the alley-
mouth with three shots before rolling to his left
without looking for a result. His gunhand swung
to the right the instant he rolled into a firing
position, and he was conscious of bullets smacking
into the hard ground around him. His eyes were
narrowed, his concentration fined down to the

single effort of getting his attacker. His thumb lifted from the hammer and the big gun blasted, emitting a flaring flash from the muzzle. The weapon jerked convulsively, kicking hard against the heel of his hand, and Devlone slitted his eyes as gunsmoke blew back into his face, its acrid stench stinging his nostrils.

He fired again, then rolled once more and waited, one shot left in his smoking gun. There was no return shooting, and he experienced a dull pang of satisfaction as he broke his gun and quickly reloaded the spent chambers. Echoes fled through the night, sullen and grumbling, and he got to one knee, checking the surrounding shadows for further hostility, reminding himself that two men had ambushed him in San Tomas the night before, and one of them was Deputy Sheriff Snark.

Satisfied that the shooting was over, he got to his feet and went to the alley, gun ready. He paused at the alley mouth but was unable to see anything in the dense shadows and turned instantly to the right, determined to discover who had been shooting at him. He reached the doorway of the store, aware that men were now emerging from the saloon, alerted by the shooting but too cautious to rush recklessly into an unknown situation.

A nearby street lamp gave him some relief, and Devlone narrowed his eyes and saw a body sprawled on the boardwalk in the store doorway. He reached it and stooped, snatching up a discarded sixgun and throwing it into the street. Covering the figure, he checked it, and grunted when he discovered the man was dead with a dark splotch of blood spreading over his shirtfront.

Excited voices caught Devlone's attention and he glanced at the saloon. Figures were emerging to cross the street. He turned and hurried to the alley, wanting to keep his identity a secret, and ran through the darkness to the back lots, hoping the ambusher who had shot at him from its cover had departed. He crashed into a corner and fell over some trash cans, sprawling headlong, then dragged himself up and went on, aware that some of the men at his back were chasing him.

A gun crashed behind him and a bullet crackled along the alley, missing by a hair's breath. He ducked and hurled himself to the left around the rear corner of the alley, his deadly gun ready in his right hand. His breath was rasping in his throat by the time he reached another alley farther along, and he traversed it to return to the street.

A crowd had gathered at the scene of the shooting, where a number of hand-held lanterns now cast yellow light into the dark corners, and Devlone listened to excited voices exclaiming about the shooting. He holstered his gun, went out to the sidewalk, and walked towards the front of the law office, where his horse was still hitched. Small groups of men were moving aimlessly around the street, some calling for information about the shooting and others already talking about lynching whoever was responsible.

'What's going on?' demanded Devlone when three men approached him as he neared the front of the jail.

'Someone killed Al Downey,' came the excited reply. 'He's lying dead in front of Lacey's Store.'

'I heard the shooting! Who was Al Downey?'

'Worked as a lawman. Sidekick to Deputy Snark.' The trio came abreast of Devlone. 'Seen anything suspicious?'

'Nope!' Devlone turned aside to untie his horse. 'Which way is the stable from here?'

'Right down the street ahead of you. On the left as you leave town.'

'Thanks!' Devlone swung into his saddle and rode at a walk along the centre of the street. He looked at the little knot of townsmen in front of the store. The sheriff was there with the town marshal at his side, and they were talking loudly. Weasel Joe Wyatt and Trig Colton were also present, and when the echoing sounds of Devlone's horse were heard, all eyes turned to survey him while a tense silence fell upon the scene.

'Hold up there, Devlone,' rapped Sheriff Ballew. 'What do you know about this, huh?'

'Me?' Devlone reined in. 'I heard the shooting, but that's common around here. Looks like you got a local epidemic of lead poisoning, Sheriff!'

He gigged his mount and rode on, ready for trouble, but the silence continued, and he breathed a little easier as he went along the street, his thoughts tight and controlled as he tried to reason out what was going on. The man he killed had been Deputy Snark's pard, and he was aware that Snark and another had ambushed him in San Tomas! He nodded thoughtfully. It was about time he questioned Snark about that incident and learned exactly what the sheriff had in mind when he ordered Snark to San Tomas to meet a man!

There was a big lantern burning over the entrance to the livery barn, and Devlone dismounted in the doorway, his ears strained for suspicious sound. The liveryman was not in evidence, and Devlone took care of his horse, letting it drink at the trough before putting it in a stall and unsaddling. He fetched a dipper filled with oats and forked hay into the rack above the animal's head before he was satisfied that the horse would survive until morning.

He was leaving the barn when hooves sounded in the street, and when he peered from the shadows he saw Hank Teasdale and Nathan Palmer leading horses towards him. Two other riders were following behind, and Devlone called to announce his presence. Both ranchers checked before coming on again.

'Say, did you hear the shooting?' demanded Teasdale.

'Yeah!' Devlone nodded. 'What happened?'

'A no-good deputy named Al Downey was killed,' said Palmer. 'I figure him and Snark set up an ambush which went wrong. Snark turned up afterwards, claiming he was at the other end of town at the time of the shooting. He ain't to be trusted, Devlone, I'm thinking.'

'I guess you're right!' Devlone nodded. 'What about your son, Teasdale? Do you figure he was telling the truth?'

'About being in town all evening?' The rancher shrugged. 'I ain't about to disbelieve him, but I sure don't like the company he's keeping, and when he turns up at the ranch I'm gonna have it out with him. He's got to toe the line like the rest of us.'

'Any idea what time they'll hold that inquest tomorrow?' asked Devlone.

'Nope. We'll check with the law office early in the morning,' answered Palmer. 'Are you sticking around town tonight?'

'Sure,' Devlone nodded. 'There are one or two things I got to look into.'

'See you tomorrow then.' Teasdale led his horse into the barn. 'Watch out for yourself, Devlone.'

'Thanks for the warning,' Devlone nodded, and Teasdale passed into the barn. As Palmer came abreast of him, Devlone reached out and gripped the rancher's arm. 'I'd like to speak to you alone,' he said in an undertone. 'I'll be along the street if you can get away from Teasdale.'

'Sure thing!' Palmer nodded. 'Give me a couple of minutes.'

Devlone walked back along the street. The crowd was thinning out now, and no lawmen were apparent. He paused in a doorway, his thoughts flitting. The silence of the night closed in as his

gaze roved around the darkened street. The door
of the law office opened briefly then banged, and a
figure materialized on the boardwalk and set off
across the street to the saloon. Devlone slitted his
eyes and recognized Town Marshal Denning's tall
figure.

Shortly, footsteps sounded to his left, coming
from the direction of the livery barn, and he
recognized Palmer as the rancher approached.
Devlone alerted the man to his presence and
Palmer came to his side.

'How can I help you?' he demanded.

'I figure to pick up Snark and question him, and
afterwards he'll be an embarrassment to me. I
need to keep my identity secret while I make an
investigation, so Snark will have to be detained in
hiding until I can arrest him openly and throw
him in the jail.'

'I could take him out to my place!' Palmer
suggested. 'I'll get a couple of my crew, who are in
town, and have them hold him out at my spread.'

'That would be fine,' Devlone nodded. 'I'll find
Snark now and take him.'

'I'll watch your movements until you've got
him,' Palmer decided, 'then fetch my men and run
Snark out to the ranch, huh?'

'That's the idea!' Devlone looked around. 'But
don't crowd me. That could prove dangerous while
someone is trying to kill me.'

'Go ahead and do what you got to and I'll watch
your back for a spell,' Palmer assured him.

'Thanks. I was hoping you'd say that!' Devlone

moved along the sidewalk to flatten himself
against the front wall of the law office. Craning
sideways, he peered inside and saw Ballew at his
desk with Snark standing before him. The sheriff
was talking animatedly, giving Snark a hard time,
for the deputy looked sullen and was shaking his
head emphatically. Devlone wished he could hear
what was being said, and settled to wait patiently.
Minutes dragged by before the deputy suddenly
shook his head, turned on his heel, and approached
the street door.

Devlone eased back into denser shadows as
Snark emerged from the office, and when the
deputy crossed the street, avoiding the saloon,
Devlone followed silently. Glancing over his
shoulder, he was pleased to see Palmer following.

Snark entered a rooming-house and ascended
the stairs with Devlone just behind. When Snark
produced a key and unlocked a door, Devlone
closed in, palming his sixgun as the deputy looked
up at him.

'Inside the room and don't make a sound!'
Devlone waggled his gun.

Snark opened his mouth to protest but thought
better of it and opened the door. The room was in
darkness and he paused, looking at Devlone.

'Stand still while I relieve you of your hardware,'
said Devlone. 'Get your hands up and don't try
anything unless you wanta join Al Downey.' He
stepped in close and snaked the man's sixgun out of
its holster. 'So far so good,' he commented. 'Now
light the lamp in the room and we'll have a talk.'

'Why are you picking on me?' demanded Snark.

Devlone laughed. 'I figure you know the answer to that. But I'll play along with you. Get the lamp lit and then we'll talk.'

Snark struck a match and entered the room. Devlone glanced along the passage and saw Palmer waiting at the top of the stairs. He nodded and the rancher departed in search of his men. With the room illuminated, Devlone entered, closing the door with his heel. He motioned with his gun and Snark crossed to the bed and sat down, fixing Devlone with a sullen, unblinking gaze.

Devlone sniffed the muzzle of the weapon he had taken from Snark and caught the unmistakable stench of recently burned powder.

'You're a mite careless, mister,' he said. 'You should have cleaned this after use.'

'I shot at a polecat earlier,' retorted Snark.

'You and Downey ambushed me earlier, like in San Tomas last night.' Devlone grinned at the expression which appeared on the deputy's face. 'No use denying it,' he added. 'I got a look at you in San Tomas, and after you lit out I saw the tracks you left and memorized them. When I checked your horse this evening I matched its damaged shoe against the picture I got in my mind. So you're in big trouble, Snark, and your best way out of this is to make a clean breast of it. You help me and I'll say a few words in the right quarter so you'll mebbe get a lighter sentence.'

'What in hell are you talking about?' blustered

Snark. 'I'm a deputy sheriff! You've got the wrong man, and you better get outa here before you wind up in a lot of trouble.'

'OK, if you wanta take that attitude!' Devlone shrugged. 'But bear in mind that men have been murdered, and you could be one of those who will feel the bite of a rope around his neck.'

'Who are you?' demanded Snark, his eyes narrowed.

'I figure you know that answer! Why did Ballew send you to San Tomas?'

'That's law business. I can't discuss it with you.'

'He said he sent you to meet a man.' Devlone nodded. 'And when you got there you ambushed me! There were two of you, so I figure the other was Al Downey. You failed in San Tomas so you tried again here, and made an even bigger mistake. Downey is dead and you're in bad trouble! So who knew I was coming up the trail?'

Snark shook his head, obstinacy showing in his face, and Devlone smiled grimly when the man remained silent.

'I've given you the chance to speak,' he said. 'And there'll be others who'll jump at the chance of saving their necks when they see the chips are down! So have it your way, Snark. I'm gonna get to the bottom of this, with or without your help. I can do it the hard way if I have to.'

'Who are you?' demanded Snark. 'Who are you working for?'

'I'm asking the questions,' countered Devlone.

Snark firmed his lips, a dogged expression

coming to his face. Devlone relaxed, holding his sixgun pointed at the floor in front of his prisoner.

'I ain't got nothing to say so what are you gonna do?' Snark grinned. 'Looks like you put yourself out on a limb, mister. There'll be big trouble around here when the sheriff finds I've gone missing.'

'You think so?' Devlone shook his head. 'I reckon Ballew will figure you've skipped the county, and he might even send a couple of men out looking for you, to shut your mouth permanently.'

Snark opened his mouth to reply, but a tap at the door stopped him and he grinned at Devlone. 'Looks like I ain't got too long to wait for help,' he grated. 'What you gonna do now, mister?'

Devlone crossed to the door and opened it with his left hand, standing to one side so he could cover the threshold and whoever was outside. A quick glance showed him Nathan Palmer waiting with two hard-bitten cowboys at his back. Palmer was holding a drawn sixgun, and smiled when he saw Devlone.

'Come in.' Devlone stepped aside, and saw Snark's expression change when the three men entered the room.

'So you got him dead to rights!' Palmer laughed harshly. 'He's cut a wide trail through this county!'

'Yeah, and he thinks he's a hard man!' Devlone shrugged. 'I figure a few days out at your place will give him time to reflect.'

'Sure. Forget about Snark until you want to talk
to him again.' Palmer waggled his gun at the
deputy. 'You're gonna take a ride with us, Snark,
and there are two ways to do it. One is to go
quietly. Or you can try the other way.'

'You won't get away with this,' Snark warned.
'The sheriff ain't stupid.'

'He must be if he relies on men like you to do his
dirty work,' retorted Palmer.

'Don't take any chances with him.' Devlone
reached for his Ranger star and held it out for
Snark to see. 'Snark, I'm arresting you on
suspicion of attempted murder, and Nathan
Palmer and his two men are empowered to hold
you prisoner until I can get back to you, so don't
give them any trouble.'

'You can rely on us, Devlone.' Palmer grinned at
Snark's discomfiture. 'Take him, men, and watch
him carefully.' He chuckled as the two men
advanced upon Snark, who sprang to his feet and
backed off.

'You won't get me out of town,' said Snark.
'There are too many men watching for trouble.'

'Just watch us!' Palmer smiled as his men
seized Snark. 'You just remember that I'll be
breathing down your neck all the way to my
ranch, and at the first sign of trouble I'll crack
your skull or split your spine with a slug. Now get
moving! Your luck has run out, Snark.'

Devlone followed as Snark was taken out, and
walked with Palmer, escorting the cowboys and
their prisoner to the livery barn. Horses were

saddled, and then the quartet rode out while Devlone stood in the shadows watching them vanish into the night before walking back along the street, pondering his next move.

He had needed some corroboration of his suspicions from Snark, for merely knowing of the man's guilt was not enough. But he figured Snark would talk after he had been given time to consider his position. So perhaps now he could run a sandy on Sheriff Ballew.

Crossing the street, Devlone paused at the batwings of Wyatt's saloon and peered in. When he saw Chick Denning inside, chatting with Weasel Joe, he glanced over at the lights in the law office and nodded slowly, dropping his hand to his holstered gun. It was time to act.

He crossed to the law office and entered, drawing his gun, his gaze on the heavy figure of the sheriff lounging at the desk. Ballew was drinking from a glass, a half-empty bottle of whiskey on the desk. Ballew looked up, his eyes narrowing.

'Why did you send Snark and Downey to San Tomas?' Devlone asked.

'What in hell has that got to do with you?'

Devlone smiled. 'I reckon you know!' he said softly. 'That's why you sent them to San Tomas, to stop me getting there. But they made a mess of it, and when they tried again tonight they came off second best.'

'You admit to shooting Downey?' demanded the sheriff.

'Yes. And before you go off half-cocked on that information you better know that I've got Snark in a safe place. He's told me everything, and I'll keep him on ice until I can put you both in a courtroom.'

Ballew had stiffened imperceptibly while Devlone was speaking, his right hand edging towards his holstered gun.

'Better not try it,' Devlone warned. 'Just lift your hands and I'll remove temptation from your hip.'

'I had you pegged for a Ranger,' said Ballew.

'And figured to have me gunned down before I arrived,' Devlone nodded. 'You're up to your neck in the crookedness around here! Ranger Headquarters notified you I was being sent into the county, huh?'

'That's about the length of the rope,' agreed Ballew. 'And you won't get away with this, Ranger. The game is too big for you to buck!'

'That ain't your concern.' Devlone waggled his gun. 'And I'm not alone in the county. Headquarters know the size of the problem and acted accordingly. Get your hands up and I'll put you where you belong.'

Ballew got to his feet, lifting his hands shoulder high. His face was set, his eyes mean-looking. But the menace of Devlone's gun held him, and Devlone took possession of the crooked lawman's Colt.

'You've got the jail keys so pick yourself a cell,' ordered Devlone. 'But I'll give you one chance to

help me pin the guilt where it belongs. If you do I
may be able to help you at your trial.'

'I got nothing to say,' Ballew sneered. 'Wait till
folks around here learn about this. Your life won't
be worth a plugged nickel.'

'Take that badge off your chest,' Devlone
rapped. 'You're an insult to every honest man who
puts his life on the line for law and order.'

Ballew flipped his badge on to the desk and
picked up the bunch of keys. He started for the
door that led into the cell block but Devlone
stopped him.

'Take off your gunbelt, then empty your
pockets,' he commanded. 'A man would be a fool to
trust you!'

Ballew reluctantly obeyed, and Devlone locked
him in a cell then returned to the office. He
produced his Ranger badge and pinned it to his
shirt front, aware that he could no longer work
under cover. The bad law set-up in the county
made it impossible for him to operate within its
protection, so he would have to do his job the hard
way....

There was a key in the lock of the street door,
and Devlone removed it, left the office and locked
the door on the outside. He paused for a moment,
but was aware that he had to act fast and went to
the hotel. The night clerk on duty looked up, noted
Devlone's arrival, and looked down again at what
he was doing, then did a double take, his face
showing surprise when he saw the silver badge
set in a silver circle on Devlone's shirtfront.

'A Texas Ranger!' he declared. 'Does Sheriff Ballew know you're in town?'

'He certainly does!' Devlone smiled. 'Is Hank Teasdale in?'

'Sure. In the bar!'

Devlone crossed to the bar and entered, looking around quickly. Half a dozen men were seated inside, and Teasdale was in the company of two others. The Tall T rancher gaped when he looked up, saw Devlone approaching, and took in the law badge.

'I see it but I don't believe it!' He got to his feet, shock apparent in his narrowed eyes.

'You better believe it,' said Devlone.

'Why didn't you tell me earlier?' Teasdale shook his head. 'I've been trying to get the Rangers into this county for a long time!'

'I need help,' said Devlone. 'I wanted to work under cover around here, but I've had to arrest Snark and Ballew so I need some special deputies.'

'Snark and Ballew under arrest?' Teasdale shook his head. 'You work fast, Ranger! But you're biting off a big mouthful, I can tell you.'

Devlone nodded. 'That's why I'm calling on you and your crew to back me.'

'You don't have to ask twice. I'll round up my crew at once.'

'Bring 'em to the law office soon as you can,' said Devlone. 'Come morning, I want the town sewn up tighter than a widow's purse, and then we can start flushing out the badmen. So get to it, and

with any luck we can have this thing beaten by
the time the sun comes up.'

The rancher nodded and departed in a rush.
Devlone turned to the door more slowly, but his
thoughts were racing. This was the critical time,
he knew, for if he did not consolidate his position
before the lawless element in the town recovered
from the setback his actions were dealing them
then he could expect big trouble, and his rashness
could well play him false and produce exactly the
opposite result he desired.

FOUR

Returning to the law office, Devlone found Chick Denning outside the building, hammering on the door with an impatient fist. The sounds echoed around the street, and the town marshal's blustering voice rasped angrily.

'Sheriff, what the hell are you doing in there? Open this damn door!'

Devlone palmed his sixgun and stuck the muzzle against Denning's ribs. The marshal froze, and Devlone relieved him of his holstered gun.

'Ballew is in a cell, Denning, and you're gonna join him!' he said. 'I figure you got enough sense to know when you're beaten.'

'What the hell!' gasped Denning. 'What's going on?'

Devlone produced the key to the door and stuck it in the lock, keeping his gun muzzle against the town marshal's ribs.

'OK, unlock the door,' he ordered, and Denning cursed as he obeyed. The door swung open and Devlone moved back a pace, letting the lamplight issuing from the office fall upon his levelled weapon. 'Inside,' he said harshly. 'Get your hands high and keep 'em up!'

Denning glanced over his shoulder and gaped at Devlone's law badge.

'Jeez!' he ejaculated. 'A Ranger!'

'That's what they tell me at headquarters.' Devlone smiled grimly.

'How come you rode into the county under cover?'

'I figure you know why! Because of the likes of you, skulking behind a law star! Take off your gunbelt.' Devlone waited until the town marshal had complied. 'Now grab the cell keys and let yourself into a cage.'

'You got nothing on me!' snarled Denning. 'My authority finishes at town limits, and I've always done my job round here.'

'If you're not actively involved in this crooked set-up then you certainly know the sheriff and his men are.' Devlone paused. 'You wanta make a clean breast of it? There's been murder committed in this county and someone will hang for that.'

'I don't know a damn thing about any of it!' Denning blustered.

'You must be blind if you didn't see anything,' insisted Devlone. 'This is clean-up time! You got anything to say before I lock you in a cell?'

'Nothing you'd believe!' Denning led the way to the cells, opened a door and entered. He gazed at Devlone while the cell door was being locked.

'I've got Snark tucked away in a hidey-hole,' said Devlone, 'and he looks the type who will holler like a stuck pig when pressure is put on him.'

Devlone went back into the office to find Teasdale and several cowboys waiting, and he arranged for the office to be manned at all times by the eager cowhands. Hank Teasdale pinned the town marshal's badge to his shirt front and strutted to and fro in the office, raising a laugh.

'It ain't no matter for laughing,' Devlone observed. 'When the brains behind this crookedness get to hear what I've done they're gonna try and do something about us. So you'd better prepare for a siege in here, and be ready to duck lead. If I can keep Ballew and Denning behind bars, one of them will crack and try to make a deal for himself. But the minute word gets out that I'm running the town someone might try to take care of your ex-lawmen.'

'Don't worry about it,' retorted Teasdale. 'We'll hold this place. Go ahead and arrest everyone mixed up in this and we'll keep 'em behind bars.'

Devlone nodded. He had started the ball rolling but had no real idea what to do next. He'd had a lucky break with the local lawmen, and while Snark was isolated out at Palmer's ranch there was every chance of breaking down Ballew's attitude and getting to the truth of the situation. But he knew it would be touch and go, and if he got it wrong in any part then he would be in big trouble.

'Hank, I saw something of the way Ballew works when we came in tonight with those two dead men,' he said. 'But what about Denning?'

'I figure Denning must have his hand in the same

barrel!' mused Teasdale. 'There's no proof against any of them, just hearsay. But you know as well as I do that there ain't no smoke without fire.'

Devlone nodded. 'We've got them both dead to rights while I can keep them apart. But I'd like to know where the town marshal stands.'

'He's a wrong 'un!' Teasdale nodded. 'And it'll come out now.'

'How do I get the deadwood on the rest of the crooked bunch? Is there any evidence against Wyatt?'

'There are plenty of pointers,' insisted Teasdale.

'Pointers ain't proof! OK!' Devlone nodded. 'So I'll have to do this the hard way! I'll start at the bottom of the pile and work up through it. But what if I find your son is mixed up in this?' He looked into the rancher's grey eyes and saw worry in their pale depths.

'My boy has always been kind of high-spirited,' Teasdale said slowly. 'But you can't pin anything on him because somebody in that raiding party laughed like he does. Hell, they could have done that on purpose, to drag us into it!'

'I'm keeping an open mind,' Devlone nodded. 'No one is gonna pin anything on anyone!' He scratched his chin. 'Maybe we can get the prominent citizens of the town together and have another town marshal elected until we know which side of the fence Denning is on. Can you contact the mayor?'

'Sure can!' Teasdale nodded. 'Seth Maxwell is OK! Leave it to me.'

'OK. Get to it.' Devlone looked at the big clock on the wall. 'I'll meet the mayor here in half an hour. Right now I got some sounding out to do. Your men will know how to act, huh?'

'Just give 'em the chance to show you!' Teasdale laughed.

Devlone left the office, and looked around into the shadows. Right now, having emerged from working under cover, he had to get around town for everyone to see him so there would be no mistake about who he was. He crossed the street and walked to the front of Wyatt's saloon to peer in over the batwings. The place was crowded almost to overflowing, and Wyatt was standing at the bar surrounded by a number of tough-looking men, Trig Colton among them. Devlone entered the saloon and paused to glance around.

He waited long enough for the occupants to notice his entrance before crossing to the bar. He asked for a beer, and was about to pay for the drink when Wyatt came to his shoulder, an ingratiating smile on his well-shaven face. Devlone was over six feet in height but he had to look up to meet the saloonman's cool gaze.

'You don't have to pay for that drink, Ranger!' Wyatt said. 'We're law-abiding citizens here and I'm pleased to see you.'

'Thanks.' Devlone threw down the price of the drink. 'But I like to buy my drinks until I get to know who's who in the place where I've come to work.'

'Suit yourself. There's nothing like being

cautious!' Wyatt's breath rasped in his massive throat, and lamplight glinted on the jewelled stickpin in his tie. 'Does Sheriff Ballew know you're a Ranger? If I recollect, you wasn't wearing that badge when you came in earlier.'

'He knows now!' Devlone smiled.

'Are you looking for anyone in particular?'

'I'm just looking over the town. There may be some owlhoots around that I know by sight.'

'There was a deputy sheriff killed about an hour ago! Are you going to look into that? Al Downey was a good man.'

'I already done something about that.' Devlone gulped his beer.

'Well if there's any way I can help you then just holler! In my business, I know just about everybody in the county. And everything is above the counter in this saloon. I employ some hard men to take care of my business interests, times being what they are, but they all act within the law.'

'I'm glad to hear it,' Devlone nodded.

Wyatt departed. Devlone gave the impression that he was relaxing, but he was tense inside, ready to flow into action. Drinking his beer, he remained alert, and noticed that a cleared space existed around him.

Wyatt moved back to his circle of hardcases, and the big saloonman spoke urgently for some minutes, while the men around him glanced at Devlone. Then the group broke up. A man went into a back room, and two others shouldered through the batwings and disappeared into the night.

Devlone finished his drink and departed quickly. On the sidewalk he pushed his back to the wall of the saloon and stood motionless while checking out the surrounding shadows. The night was cool, bright with starshine. But the shadows around the street were impenetrable. A breeze was sighing in from the range, faintly scented with the sweetness of purple sage, and silence hung like a horse blanket over the town.

He sighed and shook his head. If he could have remained under cover for a few days his job would have been a lot easier, he mused, and moved along the sidewalk, cautious and ready for action.

Returning to the sheriff's office, he found Hank Teasdale sitting at the desk in the company of a small fat man who was sweating profusely. The man was dressed in a good store suit of broadcloth and looked prosperous. He got to his feet when Devlone appeared, and waited to be introduced.

'Devlone, this is Seth Maxwell,' said Teasdale. 'He's the mayor, and owns the mercantile on Main Street. Seth, this is Ranger Devlone. He's made a good start at cleaning up around here!'

'Howdy.' Devlone shook hands. 'I guess Teasdale has been filling you in on what's being going on.'

'He has!' Maxwell's grey eyes glistened in the lamplight. 'Glad to meet you, Devlone! It's about time something was done about the set-up in this county. I've known for a long time that we had

some skunks in power around here, but there was
nothing I could do about it. So if there's anything I
can do now to help then you only got to mention it.'

'We need a new law department,' Devlone said. 'I
got evidence against Ballew and Snark that will
keep them behind bars but there's nothing against
Denning yet. So you'd better replace him. It should
be easy to get some good men sworn in.'

'Sure. No problem. Denning can be made to
resign, but the problem is finding someone suitable
to replace him.'

Devlone nodded. 'See what you can do!' he
encouraged.

Maxwell nodded and turned to the door. 'I'll get
to it right away,' he said eagerly. 'I'll send some
men over soon as I can.'

'I split my men into two groups,' Teasdale said.
'Half of them are sleeping in a couple of cells right
now, ready to take over at sun-up from the half
who'll be on duty all night. I'll leave the whole crew
with you until you get some regular lawmen in
here. I can manage for a few days if necessary. And
I'll take my son out to the ranch with me.'

'That sounds OK!' Devlone nodded. 'Fetch
Ballew out of his cell.'

Teasdale picked up the cell keys and went into
the cell block.

Devlone sat down at the desk, his thoughts
moving fast. He had to start pinning guilt where it
belonged. The sooner he could bring charges
against Ballew and put him away the easier his
task would become.

Ballew walked into the office ahead of Teasdale. The sheriff's fleshy face was taut despite his air of bravado. His eyes were narrowed, and there was a defensive light in his dark gaze which Devlone was quick to note.

'Sit down, Ballew,' Devlone snapped, and the man obeyed.

'I got nothing to say!' Ballew blustered. 'I've been doing my job to the best of my ability, and then you turn up out of the blue and throw me in jail!'

Devlone leaned his elbows on the desk. 'I need to straighten out a few things,' he said. 'When Snark returned from San Tomas you asked him why he'd been so long, and if he had made contact with the man you sent him over there to see.'

'That's right!' Ballew narrowed his eyes.

'What was the nature of Snark's trip?'

'I got a deputy down there, and Snark went to check if there had been any trouble in those parts.'

'I got a different story from Snark!' Devlone smiled.

'Where is Snark?' Ballew had tensed at the mention of the deputy, and Devlone studied the sheriff's bloated face. 'He ain't in this jail!'

'That's a fact!' Devlone nodded. 'I've put him on ice in a quiet spot because of his statement that you sent him to San Tomas to wait for and kill the Ranger on his way into this county, namely me.'

'Did Snark tell you that?' Ballew glowered. 'He must be loco!'

'Nope,' Devlone smiled. 'He saw the game was

up when I gave my facts, and decided to tell the truth, which is that he was careless in San Tomas for I got a look at him at the time of the ambush. Next day I picked up tracks of the two men who had shot at me, and followed them in this direction. I was in this office when Snark reported to you on his return from San Tomas, and I checked his horse outside and found it was one of those the two ambushers rode. When I came out of Wyatt's saloon later I was ambushed again, and I shot one of the two men involved, who turned out to be your deputy Al Downey. I picked up Snark and confronted him with these facts, and he acknowledged that they were true, which proves he ain't all loco.'

Ballew had retreated into a defensive manner while Devlone spoke, and he glared at the Ranger like a wild animal trapped in a box canyon.

'If you knew Snark better you'd realise his word don't amount to nothing.'

Devlone shook his head. 'You'll have to do better than that!'

'Well, I got nothing to say,' Ballew blustered. 'I want to see a lawyer!'

Devlone shrugged. 'Put him back in his cell, Hank!' he said. 'We'll let him sweat till morning.'

Ballew was returned to his cell, and Teasdale, when he came back to the office, cursed fitfully as he faced Devlone.

'I ain't surprised at the mess of trouble we got if what you say is true,' he observed. 'Did Ballew really send Snark and Downey to ambush you?'

'That's how it looks at the moment,' Devlone nodded. 'I'll get a signed statement from Snark tomorrow, which should clinch it. Ballew and Snark will be put away and we can get new men into the office. I need to clean up the town before I can start on the county!'

'Do you mind if I slip away now?' A harsh expression came to Teasdale's face. 'I wanta collect my boy and take him out to the ranch.'

'OK!' Devlone said. 'I can handle things around here now. Thanks for your help, and I sure as hell hope your boy ain't done anything foolish!'

Teasdale nodded and departed. Devlone got up and paced the office, his mind flitting across the broader aspects of the case. He had made a promising start, but guessed that the small fish he had netted so far made little difference to the overall situation. Someone in the county was playing for high stakes, and his hand and identity were still cunningly concealed....

He sat down again and drafted an initial report for his headquarters in Houston. As he was finishing, footsteps sounded on the boardwalk outside the office and the door was thrust open. Looking up, his hand close to the butt of his holstered gun, he saw Seth Maxwell, who was followed closely by a man who gazed with great interest at Devlone as the street door was closed.

'I've had some luck, Devlone!' Maxwell came to the desk, smiling. 'This man rode into town as I was asking questions about his whereabouts. Meet Art Stanton.' He glanced at the tall man,

who came forward with outstretched hand and a
tight smile on his lean, tanned face. 'Art, this is
Ranger Devlone.'

Stanton's handshake was firm, his blue eyes
steady, shaded by the wide brim of his grey
Stetson. He would be around thirty, Devlone
estimated, and was range-dressed: Levis and a
denim shirt open at the neck. A sixgun was on his
right hip, its holster suspended from a sagging
cartridge belt, and, although there was dust upon
his clothes, the six-shooter was spotless in its
greased holster, which was tied down by a leather
thong around his thigh.

'I'm real glad to make your acquaintance,
Devlone,' Stanton said in a low-toned voice. 'Seth
has told me what's been going on since you
arrived, and I'll be happy to step into Ballew's
boots and handle the sheriff's job.'

'Fine!' Devlone nodded. 'I need to know the town
is secure before I go out to hunt the bigger fish
that have to be caught.'

'You can forget about this place now.' Stanton
picked up the sheriff's badge and handed it to
Maxwell. 'Get the legal side of it settled, Seth, and
I'll take over. When Jackson and Bledsoe show up
I'll deputize them.'

Maxwell pinned the star to Stanton's shirtfront,
made the man raise his right hand, and got him to
repeat the oath of office. 'That makes it legal,' he
observed. 'I rooted for you at the last election, Art,
but Ballew had the county sewn up and it was no
dice. We wouldn't have had half this trouble if

you'd got in at that time.'

'Well now we got the chance to put matters right,' Stanton said firmly. He looked at Devlone, smiling faintly, and Devlone felt a load of worry lift from his mind. 'If you'll tell me what's been going on since your arrival I'll know how to handle any situation that comes up.'

'It'll be a pleasure!' Devlone said, and both Stanton and Maxwell listened intently while he gave them an account of events. When he had brought them up to date, Stanton shook his head doubtfully.

'I've had suspicions of Ballew from the moment I laid eyes on him,' he said. 'But I sure didn't think he'd stoop this low. What's your next chore?'

'I want Snark in the cells and some charges going that will put Ballew and his crooked law department out of it. Four of Hank Teasdale's cowhands are sleeping in the cells, and four more are coming in tonight to stay on guard, so you won't be short of help around here. Let's take a look at your prisoners.'

Stanton picked up the keys and led the way into the cell block. The Tall T cowhands were snoring lustily in a couple of cells, and Devlone saw Denning apparently asleep in another cell. In the end cell, Ballew was sitting on his bunk, his head in his hands. He looked up at their entrance, and turned his face to the wall when he saw Art Stanton.

They left the cowhands to snore peacefully and returned to the office. Devlone was keen to be on his way now, and took his leave, promising to return in the morning with Snark. He went out to the street, and sighed with relief as he walked along the boardwalk towards the stable. A group of men were emerging from Wyatt's saloon across the street, and two of them were arguing loudly. The group started in Devlone's direction, and he recognized Hank Teasdale, who had taken a grip upon the collar of a smaller figure. Devlone shook his head. The Tall T rancher was taking his son home!

'Howdy, Devlone,' Teasdale greeted when he reached Devlone. 'I'm taking my boy home, where he belongs. From here on in he's gonna learn to knuckle down and do his share of the chores on the ranch. His idling days are over.'

'I'm riding out your way,' Devlone replied. 'I'll side you for company.'

'Be glad to have you along!' Teasdale ordered the four accompanying cowhands to head for the sheriff's office, then escorted his unwilling son along the sidewalk and they went to the stable to saddle up their horses.

Mounted, they rode along the street towards the edge of town, and Devlone was alert, ready for trouble. He didn't think the crooked faction of the town was done with him yet, and was not surprised when a gunflash tattered the darkness of an alley mouth and raucous echoes crashed across the town.

Devlone was vacating his saddle almost before his mind registered that they were being shot at, and hit the dust on his feet, trailing his reins and drawing his sixgun as he stepped clear of his plunging horse. Then a volley of shots rang out, indicating several ambushers, and he dropped into the dust, his gun kicking against the heel of his hand as he triggered the weapon, aiming at orange flashes. His pulses raced and his heart pounded. This was where he really started earning his wages!

FIVE

Devlone blinked against the brilliant flashes stabbing at him from several points in the darkness. He was dimly aware of a horse squealing in pain, and someone to his left was also firing at the ambushers. He rolled over as bullets smacked into the ground beside him, one coming so close it kicked dust into his face. His gun blasted steadily as he returned fire, and then the fight was over. The ambushers ceased firing, and the sound of pounding feet receding away along the alley came faintly above the fading gun echoes.

Getting up, Devlone ran to the alley. But his eyes were dazzled by the shots and he was not aware of a body in front of him until he tripped over it and sprawled. Cursing, he arose, and spotted the figure of Billy Teasdale on his back, arms outflung and pale face upturned to the night sky.

'Devlone!' Hank Teasdale called hoarsely. 'How's my boy?'

Devlone dropped to one knee and examined

Billy, finding no heartbeat, his fingers encountering a wet, sticky patch on the youngster's shirtfront. His lips tightened as he arose and went to where Hank Teasdale lay.

'You been hit, Hank?' he demanded.

'Yeah, but it ain't bad enough to keep me on my back. How's my boy?'

'He's dead!' Devlone's voice was harsh. 'I'm sorry, Hank.'

'Let's get after them murderin' buzzards!' Teasdale pushed himself to his feet, then groaned, fell on his face and lay still.

Devlone looked around, his ears buzzing from the sound of the shooting. He heard voices calling along the street. Several men were running from the direction of the law office, and Devlone shouted for them to hurry. Stanton was the first to arrive, with the four Tall T cowhands close behind.

'Take care of Hank,' Devlone rapped, reloading the spent chambers of his sixgun. 'I think he's hard hit. Billy Teasdale is dead! We were ambushed from that alley mouth, and if I'm quick I might be able to pick up one of the ambushers.' He started across the street at a run, his eyes narrowed.

Gun ready, he entered the alley and flattened himself against a building. Thick shadows filled the alley and he was unable to make out details. He blinked rapidly to adjust his sight to the blackness, then started forward resolutely.

He reached the end of the alley and peered out

across the back lots. The night breeze was sighing in his ears, and he shook his head. The ambushers had disappeared as completely as if the ground had opened and swallowed them.

The sounds of tinny piano music came to his ears, and he realized he was in the alley next to Wyatt's place. Moving quickly, he hurried forward until he reached the rear wall of the saloon. Pressing in close to it, he edged along the back wall, left hand outstretched. He felt the indentation of a doorway, and his questing fingers touched a handle, which he grasped and twisted. The door opened to his touch and he entered silently and moved forward tentatively to the faint light showing around the edge of an inner door that was standing ajar.

Gun in hand, Devlone eased the door open a fraction more and craned forward to look into the main room of the saloon. The piano was silent now, and a crowd of men stood around Weasel Joe Wyatt, who was lounging with his back to the bar, his elbows propped on the polished top to support his heavy body. Two men stood before Wyatt! Both were talking rapidly, their faces hard-expressioned. One was waving a sixgun to emphasize his words and the other was clasping his right bicep. Devlone saw blood dripping from the man's sleeve and nodded. He had figured his slugs struck at least one of the ambushers.

Devlone strained his ears but could not pick out the gist of what was being said. But the scene was sufficient to warn him what was happening.

These two men had participated in the ambush
and were now reporting to Wyatt! Remaining in
cover, Devlone studied the two men, aware that
he could not go forward and arrest them for he
had no wish to put Wyatt on his guard.

Wyatt spoke, and his booming voice faintly
reached Devlone's ears. 'Hey, Taylor, you better
get yourself under cover and have that arm looked
at. Don't go to the local doc. See Jeb Swanston at
the livery barn. He's one of my men and knows a
thing or two about bullet wounds. Trask, get back
out there on the street and see what's going on
now. Act normal. A crowd'll be gathering to see
what the shooting was about so don't do anything
stupid! Just find out who's been killed and then
report back to me. And put away that damn gun!'

As the two men departed, Devlone left by the
rear and went back to the street. He paused in the
shadows and peered out to see the two men
emerging from the saloon, recognizing them by
the light issuing from the building. One of them
approached while the other turned and sneaked
off in the opposite direction. Trask walked by, and
Devlone slipped out to the sidewalk and followed
closely, easing his Colt in its holster.

A crowd had gathered around Art Stanton and
the Tall T cowhands, who were standing over the
sprawled figures of Hank and Billy Teasdale.
There was a thrill of excitement prevalent among
the townsfolk, and excited voices kept demanding
to be told what had occurred. Devlone moved
closer to Trask and stood at the man's back when

he paused to glean information. At that moment an oldish man with a black bag appeared, pushing his way through the crowd. Art Stanton immediately turned to the townsfolk.

'All right, folks,' he said. 'Break it up. Go on home. There's nothing more to see. Give the doc some space to work in!'

The crowd began to disperse, and Devlone palmed his gun as Trask turned away.

'Hold it right there, Trask!' he commanded, jabbing his muzzle against the man's spine. 'That's a gun muzzle you're feeling. I got you dead to rights. Just stand still. Don't put your hands up, and don't make any sudden movements! Let's wait until the crowd has gone before we talk.'

The man stiffened, and turned his head to peer at Devlone.

'The Ranger!' he said with a curse.

'You got it right first time!' Devlone smiled. 'Just be patient and you'll get the chance to talk when the crowd has gone.'

The townsfolk dispersed quickly, and Art Stanton turned to Trask, unable to see Devlone and his gun.

'What's wrong with you?' he demanded. 'Didn't you hear what I said? Get off the street or I'll throw you in jail.'

'I want you to do just that with this one, Art!' Devlone replied. 'Disarm this galoot and check his gun for evidence. He was in the ambush.'

Stanton relieved Trask of his gun and sniffed the muzzle, grimacing at the reek of recently burned powder. He stuffed the weapon into his waistband and called over two of the four Tall T cowhands standing nearby before looking at Devlone.

'This weapon has been fired recently,' he agreed. 'Within the last few minutes, I judge. How'd you drop on to this jasper?'

Devlone explained tersely, his harsh voice grating in the night, and, when he lapsed into silence, Stanton nodded grimly.

'Take this guy to the jail and lock him in a cell,' he told the two cowhands. 'Don't let him talk to anyone on the way.'

The man was seized and bundled away along the street. Devlone tried to relax. He looked at Stanton's shadowed face.

'What do you wanta do about Wyatt?' Stanton demanded.

'Nothing at the moment.' Devlone was thinking fast. 'Let him sweat. When Trask doesn't report back Wyatt'll start wondering where in hell he's got to, and he'll make a bee-line for another jasper named Taylor, who took a slug in the arm in the shooting and is on his way to see a man called Swanston at the livery barn to get patched up. We better collect Taylor now.'

'You bet!' Stanton said eagerly.

At that moment the doctor got to his feet from Hank Teasdale's side.

'Hank is in a real bad way!' he reported. 'It'll be touch and go. I'll have him taken down to my place, but the move could kill him.'

'Keep us informed about his condition,' Stanton said. 'Thanks, Doc.'

'Let's get on to the livery barn,' suggested Devlone. 'Maybe we can make something out of this development.'

Stanton agreed and they walked along the street. Devlone glanced at Wyatt's saloon in passing. A figure was inside, looking out over the batwings.

'Down this alley,' Stanton said suddenly. 'We better not walk in the front door if we wanta catch someone in the act.'

They went on in silence, traversed an alley and turned left to approach the livery barn from the rear. Stanton led the way, and Devlone was at his shoulder as they went through a back doorway. They passed between two rows of horses tethered in stalls. There was an office down at the street end of the barn, and lamplight filtered out through a half-open door.

Stanton pushed open the office door and they went straight in. Taylor was sitting at the desk, his shirt removed, and a tall, thin man was bending over him, examining a bullet wound high up in Taylor's arm.

'I'd better get some hot water,' Swanston was saying when he became aware of the arrival of the two lawmen. He straightened and swung round to face the door, and Devlone palmed his sixgun as the liveryman's right hand made an instinctive movement to the gun holstered on his right hip.

'You better not try that!' Devlone said harshly,

and the liveryman froze. Taylor looked up quickly, and shock filled him when he saw the lawmen. His already pale face turned haggard and his shoulders slumped. 'That's right,' Devlone continued. 'Taylor, you're under arrest for being involved in the murder of Billy Teasdale, and there may be other charges brought against you. Swanston, I'm arresting you on a charge of aiding a wanted man, knowing him to be involved in criminal activities. That will hold you until we find out exactly what your relationship is with Joe Wyatt.'

'Just a minute!' Swanston snarled. 'I don't know nothing from nowhere! I don't even know this man! He came in here bleeding and I was just trying to help him!'

'And you didn't even hear this shooting in town a few minutes ago, huh?' demanded Devlone. 'Save your protests till later, mister. You'll get a chance to state your case but now ain't the time for it. Let's go. You know where the jail is.'

Taylor began to proclaim his innocence, claiming he had been hit by a stray bullet in the shooting in passing and had wandered into the barn hoping to be directed to the doctor's office. Stanton dragged the man to his feet, snatched his sixgun from its holster and sniffed the muzzle. He turned and stuck the weapon under Devlone's nose.

'You reckon this gun has been fired recently?' he demanded.

'In the last few minutes, I'd say!' Devlone

nodded. 'Save your story for later, Taylor. We got work to do!'

They walked to the jail and the prisoners were locked in a cell. Devlone stood in the office wondering what to do next. Stanton came in from the cells, jangling the bunch of keys, and looked enquiringly at Devlone.

'If we go on as we have been doing we're gonna need more cells,' Stanton observed. He put the bunch of keys on the desk. 'What happens now? Can we do something about Wyatt?'

'You figure he's the kingpin behind the trouble?' countered Devlone.

'Who else?' Stanton shrugged. 'The bad trouble only started when he moved into town. Before he came in off the range the place was OK.'

'What do you mean by that?'

'Wyatt bought the JW ranch about five years ago, and bad things started happening out there – rustling, trouble over range rights. Then a stagecoach was robbed of about twenty thousand dollars and suddenly Wyatt bought that saloon and began to expand in town. Now he owns the livery barn Swanston runs, and he's got an interest in the store that opened up in opposition to Seth Maxwell.'

Devlone frowned as he digested the information. 'So it looks as if we've got to try and get evidence against Wyatt, and it'll have to be water-tight.' He glanced at the clock on the wall. 'I need to pick up Snark and get him to talk. If we put the heat on Ballew he'll start spilling his guts

about the next guy, and it will go on right through
the whole crooked bunch until it reaches the boss.
So you better take statements from these
prisoners. Come morning, they're all gonna be
screaming for a lawyer, and I don't want any of
them out on the street until I got a case against
whoever is organizing the crime in this county.'

'That's a good idea!' Stanton nodded. 'I'll get on
with the paperwork while you bring Snark in.'

'Let's hope I can get out of town without more
shooting!' Devlone turned to the door then
paused. 'Can you give me directions for Palmer's
ranch? I came to town from there by way of the
Tall T, and I don't need to ride all over the range
retracing my steps.'

Stanton obliged, and Devlone went to saddle up
and ride out, making for Nathan Palmer's Broken
P ranch. Hitting the open trail, he let the horse
stretch out, his thoughts fast and furious. The
dead wood had been stripped from the local law,
and, if he moved fast, he should be able to settle
the trouble without too much difficulty....

He had no trouble finding the Broken P ranch,
and grunted in relief when the spread appeared
before him in the indistinctness of pre-dawn. He
rode on openly, and had reached a gate leading
into the yard when a low voice challenged him
from nearby shadows. He reined up and a guard
appeared, carrying a levelled rifle.

'Howdy,' Devlone greeted.

'Howdy, Ranger,' came the quick reply. 'You've
come for Snark, I guess. He's in the bunkhouse

with a man guarding him.'

Devlone glanced around. The ranch house was in darkness, and there was a faint yellow glow at the window in the bunkhouse. 'I don't need to wake up the whole spread,' he decided. 'If you could saddle up Snark's horse I'll get him out of the bunkhouse and be on my way.'

'The boss wouldn't want to miss you,' said the guard. 'He had a lot of good things to say about you when he got back from town last night. It might be more than my job is worth to let you ride out without passing the time with Nathan!'

'I'm in a hurry. Working against the clock!' Devlone gigged his mount towards the bunkhouse. 'I'd like to be back in town in time for breakfast.'

'Then you've got some hard riding to do.' The guard started across the yard to the barn. 'I'll throw a saddle on Snark's hoss!'

Devlone entered the bunkhouse to find a cow-hand drowsing at a table, a rifle across his knees. He jerked up as Devlone opened the door, and rubbed his eyes tiredly when he saw the law star on Devlone's chest.

'Snark?' Devlone demanded.

The guard jerked a thumb at a nearby bunk. 'That damn skunk has been snoring all night long,' he complained. 'Be glad to see you haul him out of here.'

Devlone crossed to the bunk and grasped Snark's shoulder, shaking him several times before the man came to his senses. He sat up, and scowled when he recognized Devlone.

'Come on, Snark,' Devlone told him. 'You're going back to town.'

'Hell, can't it wait till morning?' Snark protested.

'You'll get all the sleep you want in a cell,' Devlone retorted. 'But you won't feel so relaxed when we get back to town, the trouble I've been dealing with and the men I've arrested.'

'You ain't got nothing on me!' Snark growled.

'You figure Ballew is gonna take the rap for what you did, huh?'

'What do you mean?' Suspicion glimmered in Snark's eyes.

'I got Ballew in a cell, along with Denning, and they're facing charges which might put a rope round their necks. Before I left town to fetch you in, Ballew hinted that he was ready to do a deal. He's ready to throw you to the wolves in return for a lighter sentence for himself. You ambushed me twice in two days, and the Rangers don't like it when one of their men get shot up. They'll sure make an example of you, Snark!'

'Ballew can't get away with that! He's the sheriff and I'm only a deputy! Anything I ever did was on his say-so! What are you trying to pull?'

'Nothing!' Devlone shook his head. 'It don't matter none to me who goes inside so long as I get the guilty men. But I can see that crooked sheriff is gonna pull some strings to stay out of jail, him being another who don't give a cuss who takes the rap so long as it ain't him!'

'I'll tell you what was going on around this

county before you showed.' Snark was rigid in his bunk. 'Ballew got mixed up in every crooked scheme that came along. He got a rake-off from the bank robbery, and he had the idea that the Rangers would send a man into the county under cover. He sent me to San Tomas to watch for the State Law.'

'You make a statement to that effect and maybe we can get Ballew to do his own time in prison,' Devlone prompted.

'You're damn right I wanta make a statement! I'll take the lid off the tricks that have been pulled around here!'

'I can't believe Ballew is the top man in the bad bunch. He don't look the type who could organize it. Is he taking orders from someone?'

'Sure he is!' Snark laughed. 'But it's more than my life is worth to open my trap about that. I'd rather go to prison for ambushing you than take a chance of staying in the clear by talking out of turn against the big boss. I wouldn't live two minutes after pointing the finger in court.'

'I got my own ideas about who the man is,' Devlone observed. 'And you don't know what's been happening around town! Billy Teasdale was gunned down and Hank Teasdale stopped lead and has only a fifty-fifty chance of making it through the night. Taylor and Trask are in jail for doing the shooting, and they'll start spilling the beans soon as they know they're likely to hang for what they did. Maybe you're lucky to have been under arrest.'

'You're putting me on, Ranger!' Snark shook his head. 'You're trying to scare me! Well, I don't scare easy, see! Take me back to town and throw me in the hoosegow! I'll take what's coming to me!'

'OK!' Devlone nodded. 'Sit down at the table and we'll get that in writing. It'll put you in the clear as far as the other crimes are concerned, and it will give me a lever against Ballew.'

'I ain't too keen about having my words put on paper!' Snark said warily.

'It's the only way to ensure that you don't get blamed for things you didn't do! When Ballew and Denning start talking they're gonna clear the air considerable, and you can bet they'll go easy on themselves.'

'OK, I'll tell you what I know, and you better believe that Denning heard the orders Ballew gave me about nailing you!'

'So put it in your statement and I'll confront Denning and Ballew with the evidence.' Devlone sat down at the table, motioning for Snark to sit opposite. He reached into his breast pocket and produced some writing paper and a pencil, and induced Snark to give an account of Ballew's orders concerning the ambushes. Afterwards Snark signed the statement and Devlone had the watching cowhand witness it. 'Now we'll go back to town,' Devlone said.

'You'll have to keep Ballew away from me,' Snark said uneasily.

'Don't worry!' Devlone smiled. 'I'll watch over you like a father!'

They went outside and Devlone roped Snark in
his saddle. There was a red glow in the eastern
sky as they rode away from the ranch, and
Devlone glanced around. Time was fleeting, and
right now he wished he could be in two places at
once. But he figured events in town would hang
fire until he returned, and settled himself to the
long ride. Tiredness was clawing at his mind, but
he remained alert as they continued, aware that
desperate men were likely to try desperate
measures when the chips were down.

Snark drowsed in his saddle as they continued,
and soon the sun cleared the horizon and killed off
the remaining shadows. Devlone let his mind flit
over the broad face of the situation now facing
him, trying to make tentative plans on the best
way to bring the case to a successful conclusion.

About an hour after they had left the Broken P
a rifle cracked from somewhere behind them,
flinging a string of echoes to the distant horizon.
Devlone grabbed his Winchester from its boot and
dived out of his saddle, hitting the ground on his
feet and running to Snark's side, for the man was
hog-tied and unable to move. But Snark was
beyond aid, lolling against the rope that bound
him, a spreading stain of blood on his shirtfront.
He had been shot in the back and the bullet had
dusted him both sides!

Devlone turned grimly and looked along his
back trail. He saw drifting gunsmoke about 200
yards behind, marking a clump of brush as the
ambush spot. Trailing the reins of Snark's horse

and leaving it standing, he swung back into his saddle and rode fast for the ambush spot, his rifle ready across his thighs. He wanted the killer who had shut Snark's mouth....

Teeth clenched, Devlone knee'd his horse forward. He lifted his rifle, covering the ambush spot, and hammered up an incline. But nothing happened, and he jumped the patch of cover from which the shot had been fired and swung his horse about, dismounting swiftly and dropping into a firing position. He twisted around, slitted eyes looking for movement, and his teeth clicked together when he spotted a rider high-tailing it across the lower stretch of a slope which declined away from the rear of the ambush spot.

Devlone ran to his horse and took a pair of field glasses from his saddlebag. He adjusted the glasses but barely had time to focus on the rider before he rode into trees and was lost to sight. But one glimpse was enough to give Devlone an image of a tall scarecrow of a man dressed in Levis and a black shirt, with a battered black Stetson pulled down low over long, lank fair hair. The horse was brown, its left foreleg white from fetlock to knee.

Returning the glasses to his saddle-bag, Devlone mounted and set off in pursuit. He pushed his horse fast, noting that they were riding west, and from time to time caught a fleeting glimpse of his quarry. The ambusher was not in any great hurry. Devlone made up some ground on him, but was not keen to take him immediately, being more interested at this stage in learning who the killer was working for. If he could trace the ambusher back to the man who had ordered Snark's death then real progress would be made.

But as Devlone approached a stand of timber on the trail of the ambusher, a puff of gunsmoke erupted from cover ahead and a rifle bullet smashed into the chest of his horse, dropping it with a squeal of pain and threshing legs. He barely had time to kick his feet free of the stirrups before he hit the ground, and had to roll desperately to avoid being crushed by the animal.

Devlone snaked in behind the horse, expecting a shot to take him out, but silence ensued, and he realized that his death was not on the cards. The killer was not prepared at this moment to kill a Texas Ranger!

SIX

Devlone drew his Winchester and cocked it before peering over his horse to check out the ambush spot. He saw no sign of his quarry. At one hundred yards from the spot where the shot had been fired, he knew that if the killer was still crouching there then he would be dead before he could move a couple of yards. Removing his hat, he offered it up as a target but nothing happened and he realized he would have to do it the hard way.

The ambusher had aimed at his horse rather than at him, which indicated that the intention had been to dismount him rather than to kill. He steeled himself for the effort and sprang up. Gaining his feet in a swift movement, he started running towards the ambush spot.

Muscles tensed, Devlone waited for the inevitable! But there was no impact of a bullet striking his body. Silence had closed in about him, and he ran and ducked and zig-zagged, his rifle ready, his gaze centred upon the spot from which the shot had come. His breath rasped and he sweated, but kept moving, and tense moments later he reached the ambush spot and dropped flat, his shoulders heaving and sweat running into his eyes.

For a time he lay gasping, soaked in sweat, but by degrees his breathing returned to normal and he eased himself into a sitting position. The first thing he saw, glinting in the bright sunlight, was an ejected 30-30 cartridge case, and he snatched it up, noting two parallel scratches on it which denoted a faulty extractor. He fingered the scratches, then dropped the cartridge case into a pocket.

He looked for tracks and saw his ambusher's hoofprints leading off into the distance. Wiping his forehead on his sleeve, he heaved a sigh. Now he was in a fix! He returned to where his horse had fallen, and anger filled him as he looked at the dead animal. Turning away, he began to walk resolutely back to where he had left Snark dead in his saddle, telling himself that his turn would come....

It took him a long time to reach Snark. The horse was casually cropping grass with the dead man still lolling grotesquely in the saddle as he had at the moment the ambusher's bullet let daylight through him. Devlone untied the rope supporting the corpse, lowered it to the ground, and left it wrapped in a blanket. He thankfully swung into the saddle and wearily returned the few miles to his own mount, only too aware that tiredness was crowding his mind for he had not closed his eyes during the previous night. He resaddled with his own gear and rode on, picking up the ambusher's trail and following carefully, aware that at any moment another shot could blast at him. But he pushed on, following tracks, his mind niggling at the situation that was evolving.

What he could not understand was where the ambusher had come from and how he had known they would be out riding at that exact time. And apart from that, why had Snark been killed? The questions baffled him, but he meant to have the answers. The ambusher himself knew those answers so he had to be taken and made to talk....

When the tracks petered out on rocky ground, Devlone dismounted and cast around, but was unable to pick up further sign of his quarry. He found soft ground again, but there was nothing to indicate which way the ambusher had ridden. He put himself in the ambusher's place and tried to work out what the man would have done. But no bright ideas presented themselves to his questing mind and he found himself at a loss. The ambusher had vanished as if he had suddenly sprouted wings.

There was only one thing for it, Devlone realized. He would have to return to the spot where Snark's body lay and try to back-track the ambusher, for the man might not have been so careful with his trail before the shooting, and if it was possible to read his former movements from his tracks then Devlone might get some answers to the questions bothering him.

He stifled his impatience and again returned to

where Snark's body lay on the hard ground. With scarcely a glance at the grim sight, he went to the ambush spot and immediately found the killer's tracks made before the shooting. Back-tracking patiently, he discovered that the ambusher had ridden along the tracks he and Snark had made from the Broken P, and, when the ranch came into sight, Devlone rode around it in a half-circle following the unknown killer's trail. Satisfying himself that the killer had come from the direction of Ash Bend, and picking up the trail that retraced his own ride towards the town with Snark, he broke off to return to Palmer's ranch.

It was midday. The sun blazed down from high overhead and the breeze was like the draught from an oven. Devlone eased himself in his saddle and crossed Palmer's yard. As he dismounted, the rancher emerged from his house and stood regarding him in surprise. Devlone wrapped his reins around the hitchrail and stepped on to the porch to move into the surrounding shade.

'I heard you called and took Snark,' Palmer said. 'But you ain't been to town and returned in the time you've had. Did you find trouble on the trail?'

'You could say that!' Devlone explained tersely what had occurred and Palmer's grizzled face evinced shock.

'Hell, I would've sent some men along if I'd thought this might happen,' he growled. 'What can I do to help?'

'I'm plumb tuckered out!' Devlone replied. 'I

could do with a square meal and some coffee.
Then someone could pick up Snark's body, take it
into town and explain to Art Stanton what
happened. I've got tracks to follow and there ain't
no telling where they might lead me.' He paused,
considering the situation, then sighed deeply. 'On
second thoughts, maybe you'll bring Snark's body
back here and hide it until we can get round to
giving him a decent burial. He's still an
embarrassment, and I'd like the news on his
death delayed until I've got a clearer picture of
what's going on. Can you do that?'

'Sure thing!' Palmer nodded. 'I'll fetch him in
myself so no one can talk about it. Did you get a
look at the killer? Maybe I could identify him if I
knew what he looked like.'

Devlone described the man, and Palmer shook
his head.

'Nope,' he declared. 'That don't start no wheels
turning in my head. What about his horse?'

'It was brown, with the left foreleg white from
fetlock to knee.'

Palmer grimaced. 'That covers a lot of horses on
this range,' he opined.

'Yeah, but I'll know the animal again if I see it,
and the man,' Devlone declared.

He had a meal at the ranch then set off again,
fighting his tiredness. Returning to the
ambusher's trail, he checked it again, noting faint
details about the tracks that would distinguish
them from a hundred others. He rode carefully, his
gaze on the ground and lifting only occasionally to

take in the country into which they were heading.
As far as he could tell the tracks were coming from
Ash Bend, and he wondered how the killer had
fallen in with him. He had obviously intended to
kill Snark, and had done so with one bullet, and
he'd had plenty of opportunities to shoot Devlone
himself.

As far as Devlone knew, Ballew was the only
one who would benefit from Snark's death! But
the crooked sheriff was in jail and no one outside
the law office could have contacted him. Yet there
was a possibility that Wyatt had put a man to
watching Devlone and to kill Snark when the
chance presented itself. If Wyatt was the brain
behind the crookedness then he would want to
protect his links in order to cover himself.

It was mid-afternoon when Devlone sighted Ash
Bend, and the tracks he was following were still
easy to read. They led straight into the stable,
and, thinking of Jeb Swanston, whom he knew to
be Wyatt's man, he wondered if there was a
connection. Dismounting in the yard, he took care
of the horse, put it in a stall with feed, and then
looked around, checking out the horses in the
barn in case the killer had circled and ridden back
to town ahead of him. But he found nothing
resembling the horse he had seen on the range
and went into the dusty office, where an old man
was sitting at a battered desk.

'Are you in charge here now Swanston's in jail?'
Devlone demanded.

'Sure am! Jake Bindon's my name.'

'Have you come in to take care of things because Swanston is in jail or do you normally work here?'

'I've took care of the hosses around here for more than twenty years!'

'Know someone who owns a brown horse with a white left foreleg?'

'White left foreleg?' Bindon screwed up his seamed face as he considered. 'Nope,' he declared. 'That could fit a dozen horses I've seen around here.'

'Make a list of every man you know who rides such a horse,' Devlone told him. 'And while you're at it, bear in mind that the rider is a tall scarecrow of a man with long, fair hair, wearing a black shirt and a black hat.'

'What's this jasper done, Ranger?'

Devlone grimaced. 'Nothing that I know of. I saw him at a distance on the range and figure he might be my brother!' He smiled and moved to the door. 'I'll call back for that list in about an hour.'

Going out to the street, Devlone paused to get his first daylight look at Ash Bend, his expression harsh as he noted Wyatt's saloon and recalled the incidents that had occurred in the shadows around the street during the night. He saw a gunsmith's sign and was reminded of the ambusher's cartridge case in his pocket. He walked along to the gun shop and entered, producing the rifle shell when a small, fat man appeared from the rear of the shop.

'Howdy!' Devlone greeted, holding out the cartridge case. 'I'm Brad Devlone, Texas Ranger.'

'Sure! I heard of you! I'm Ike Carson. What can I do for you?'

'Take a look at this.'

The man examined the case. 'Sure! Faulty extractor! The weapon will eventually jam, so if it's yours, bring it in and I'll look at it.' Brown eyes lifted from the cartridge case to gaze at Devlone's Ranger badge. 'It could be fatal for a man in your business to have a faulty extractor! When it fails it will be sudden, no warning. The extractor will break!'

Devlone nodded. 'Yeah. I know! It happened to me once on the Mexican Border! Keep that shell in a safe place until I return with another to match it! I'm looking for the man who ejected it after ambushing me. So if anyone brings in a jammed Winchester, let me know about it, huh?'

'Sure thing!' Carson nodded. 'Anything for the law!'

Devlone went outside and stood on the sidewalk, not certain that he had accomplished much. He went along to the law office, fighting tiredness, aware that his need for sleep was becoming crucial. Now was the time to take a rest, he knew, for there were a few hours yet before darkness came, and nothing much should happen while the honest folk of the town were about their normal business!

He went into the law office, determined to settle the question of Sheriff Ballew's guilt, and Art Stanton looked up tiredly from the desk where he sat.

'Where's Snark?' he demanded when Devlone closed the door.

'I decided to leave him where he is!' Devlone handed Snark's statement to Stanton, remaining silent while the new sheriff read it.

'That will keep Ballew where he belongs,' Stanton said at length. 'I'll get him out here. If he makes a statement now we'll have a case.'

Devlone nodded. 'What about Hank Teasdale?'

'He's still hanging in there. Got a good fifty-fifty chance, the doc says.'

Devlone sat down beside the desk, stifling a yawn and trying to relax. Stanton returned, herding Ballew in from the cell block, and the crooked sheriff paused and gazed at Devlone as if the sight of him was a bad dream.

'Where's Snark?' Ballew demanded aggressively.

'I'm keeping him on ice until your trial! I don't want anything happening to him before he stands up in court to spill his guts about you.'

'Snark is lying to save himself. He got caught up in the crime hereabouts, and used a trip I sent him on to ambush you without my knowledge.'

'You knew he turned renegade, and did nothing about it?' Stanton cut in.

'I was hoping he'd lead me to bigger game!' Ballew breathed heavily, as if he could already feel the bite of a hemp necktie around his throat.

'You got any ideas about the man Snark was working for?' Devlone asked.

Ballew shook his head. His bloated face was

grey, and his eyes were filled with real fear. Sweat beaded his forehead and his hands trembled. He drew a deep breath, then exhaled slowly.

'I been working the county alone for a long time,' he said. 'Too much for one man! And I had to use what men I could get. I couldn't trust Snark further than I could spit. And Al Downey throwed in his hand with Snark!'

'Downey was the deputy I killed when he and Snark ambushed me on the street, huh?' mused Devlone. 'So they were crooked, and you didn't turn up a thing against them.' He shook his head. 'Do you figure a jury will believe that story? Especially with Snark's evidence against you?'

'They'll take my word against Snark's! I've been the sheriff for a lot of years! Snark ain't never been anything than a two-bit lawman!'

'I was in here when Snark returned from San Tomas,' Devlone said. 'And I heard every word you said to him. With my evidence backing Snark's, you don't have a prayer!'

'You can't swing it. You'd do better making a deal with me.'

'So what have you got to offer?' asked Stanton.

'I learned some things in the past week!' Ballew retorted. 'Turn me loose and I'll fix it for you to meet someone. I'll talk to him with you on hand to hear what he says, and he'll open up. That should be good enough to rope him in and some more of his pards.'

Devlone shook his head. 'Give me some hard facts now and I'll consider a deal. I reckon I got you dead to rights anyway, so if you wanta take a chance with your neck then that's up to you! Put him back in his cell, Art! We'll let him stew a little longer! He knows that if I make a breakthrough without his help then he can't get himself a deal, and one fine morning they'll take him out of here and stretch his neck with a new rope.'

Ballew narrowed his eyes at Devlone's grim words but turned to re-enter the cell block, and Stanton ushered him out. Devlone leaned back in his seat to consider what had been said, sensing that Ballew was still a long way from breaking. When Stanton returned, Devlone got to his feet.

'I got to hit the sack for a few hours,' he said. 'I ain't closed my eyes since I hit this county. It sure is hell on lawmen around here, huh?'

'Yeah,' Stanton nodded. 'Mebbe you better tell me where you got Snark holed out. If something happened to you I'd need to bring him in.'

'He'll keep.' Devlone walked to the street door. 'What about Denning? We can't hold him without bringing charges.'

'It might be a good idea to turn Denning loose tonight and trail him. He's sure as hell gonna contact his crooked pards the minute he's able to!'

'You could be right. It's beginning to look like we'll have to force this business!' Devlone opened the door. 'I'll talk to you later. I'll be on the street again about sundown.'

He went back to the stable to confront the ostler, and Jake Bindon looked at a piece of paper on which he had written some names.

'You know, Ranger, there ain't so many hosses around like you describe.'

'That's what I figured,' Devlone grinned.

'There's Bill Nolan out at Lazy T. He's got a brown hoss with one white leg. But I can't remember if that's front or back.'

'What does Nolan look like?'

'Big guy. Maybe two hundred pounds. Got a spade beard nigh black as midnight.'

'He ain't the one I'm looking for! Who else?'

'Tom Ellins! But I got a feeling his hoss has two white legs! Could you be mistaken about that animal you seen?'

'Nope. It had one white leg!'

'Ellins is old, mebbe sixty. Say, you got Ballew jailed! What's he done?'

'We don't know yet! You got anyone else on that list?'

'Frank Wilson! But I recollect his bronc busted a leg and was shot! You should talk to Ira Rosenbloom! He's been saying Ballew is crooked but no one believed him, being the town drunk an' all!'

'Where does Rosenbloom hang out?'

'Joe Wyatt's saloon. Does odd jobs around the place for food and drink. Mind you, he don't talk a lot of sense these days. Rotgut's got at his brains!'

'Thanks for the information.' Devlone turned to leave.

'Wish I could've been more help, Ranger!'

Devlone departed and paused on the street, eyes raking his surroundings. He turned his steps

to Wyatt's saloon and pushed through the
batwings, stepping to one side of the door and
looking around. There were fewer patrons at this
time of the afternoon, although a big poker game
was going on at a corner table. There was no sign
of Weasel Joe Wyatt, but some hardcases were
present, and the ominous figure of Trig Colton
was isolated at the far corner of the bar, near the
foot of the stairs leading to the upper rooms.

Colton was regarding Devlone, his right hand
down near the butt of his holstered Colt .45.
Devlone returned the unblinking scrutiny. Colton
was dressed in black pants and a black shirt,
black neckerchief and a black Stetson. He was a
striking figure in his sombre dress, and his
hawk-like features were completely devoid of
emotion. Devlone had heard stories about Colton
but the man was not wanted by the law so far as
he knew.

Devlone went to the bar and crooked a finger at
the bartender. 'Beer!' he said, feeling in his pocket
for a coin.

'Your money's no good in here, Ranger!' Colton's
sharp voice cut through the atmosphere. 'Joe
Wyatt says anything you want is on the house.'

'Thanks, but I always pay for my own drinks,'
Devlone replied, tossing a silver dollar on the bar
top.

'Suit yourself!' Colton shrugged.

Devlone sank his beer and wiped his mouth on a
dusty sleeve. He picked up his change, and paused
to fix the bartender with a hard gaze.

'Where does Ira Rosenbloom hang out when he's not in here?' he asked.

'You'll find him sleeping it off in a shack back of Swanston's stable.'

Devlone departed. The afternoon sun was almost too bright for his tired eyes and he glanced longingly in the direction of the hotel halfway along the street. Acting on an impulse, he went to the hotel and signed in, intending to see Rosenbloom, pick up his gear at the stable, then turn in. As he turned from the desk a woman called him, and he saw Rana Teasdale descending the stairs. He had forgotten about her in the press of the situation, and noted her shocked face and wide eyes. She was wearing Levis and a red checked shirt, carrying a low-crowned plains hat in one hand.

'How is your father now, Miss Teasdale?' he demanded.

'He's holding his own!' She spoke in a clipped tone, her lips tremoring. 'Have you jailed the man responsible?'

'I got two men behind bars. Taylor and Trask. They were involved.'

'They're only the men who did it! I'm talking about the snake who stands to gain from my pa's death.'

'If there is someone else involved I won't rest until he's in jail.' Devlone stifled a yawn, aware that he wouldn't sleep peacefully until something broke in his favour.

'You don't need to look further than Joe Wyatt!'

There was venom in her voice, and Devlone looked into her face, aware that she was overwrought. Her hands were trembling, her fingers mashing the hard brim of her hat.

'Why do you accuse Wyatt?' he countered.

'He's been pestering my father for months, wanting to buy the Tall T! And when Pa wouldn't sell bad things began to happen around the place. A water-hole got poisoned and we lost stock! Some of our men were scared off the range! Billy was caught up in bad company! And they finally killed him! What more do you need to know about Wyatt?'

'You got any proof to back up your accusations?'

'You've only got to ask to find other people Wyatt has been stomping.'

'Name some! I'm a stranger in the county and nobody is talking to me. Give me some hard facts, or put me in touch with someone who can.'

'Wyatt's got everyone so scared they daren't talk! Even my pa kept his mouth shut until it was too late!'

'Just point me in the direction of someone who might be able to prove something!' Devlone spoke quietly, aware that the hotel clerk was leaning on his desk and listening intently. 'Are you just leaving the hotel? I got some business along the street. Take a walk with me.'

He opened the street door and stepped aside for her to precede him, then joined her on the sidewalk, his mind racing with conjecture. All he needed was one shred of evidence against the man behind the trouble and the whole construction of crookedness would collapse like a house built of playing cards. He threw an all-seeing glance around the street and chill shock ran through him when he saw a man step into view from behind a wagon across the rutted street. Simultaneously a quick movement at the other end of the wagon caught his attention, and he glimpsed the tell-tale glint of sunlight on a drawn weapon.

'Quick, back into the hotel!' Devlone thrust the girl out of the doorway, drew his Colt and hurled himself to the sidewalk. The next instant the front of the hotel was blasted by questing lead, and he felt the flashing bite of a bullet somewhere in his left leg below the knee. Then his big gun was bucking and smoking, blasting raucously as he threw hot lead back across the street in a furious exchange that would obviously end in death for someone!

SEVEN

Devlone triggered his Colt as he rolled to the left
on the rough boardwalk, the thick stench of acrid
gunsmoke in his nostrils. His concentration had
fined down to the two figures behind the wagon
opposite, and his second bullet took the ambusher
on the left in the chest. The man threw down his
gun and jack-knifed away from the wagon.
Devlone switched his attention to the second man,
who was using a rifle, and ducked as a 30-30
bullet tore through the crown of his hat. He rolled
to the right, triggering his Colt as he came up into
the aim on his elbows. The bullet took the
ambusher in the throat and hurled him four feet
backwards to lie crumpled in the dust.

Devlone grunted in pain as he pushed himself
upright. The dying echoes of the shooting were
growling away into the distance as he leaned
against an awning post and reloaded his Colt. He
saw men running forward, attracted by the disturbance, and Art Stanton was one of the foremost.

'Are you bad hurt?' Rana Teasdale appeared at
Devlone's side.

'I don't think so.' There was pain in Devlone's left leg and he looked down at his riding boot. A gouge showed where a slug had penetrated, and he stuck a finger in it and found a sticky patch of blood but no bullet hole as such. There was another gouge at the back of the boot where the bullet had made an exit. 'Just a bullet burn, I guess,' he observed, putting his foot back on the ground and stamping to test its efficiency. Pain stabbed through his limb and he gritted his teeth. 'I reckon it'll carry me!' He paused. 'I don't know if that ambush was meant for you or me!'

Her eyes widened at the import in his words, then she went back into the hotel. Devlone crossed the street to where Stanton was bending over the one of the two bodies.

'He's dead!' Stanton straightened as Devlone reached him.

'Any idea who he is?'

'No, but I've seen him hanging out at Wyatt's place. Are you OK?'

'Just about! Let's take a look at the second guy!'

They walked around the wagon and Stanton examined the other ambusher. The man was also dead, and Devlone recognized his taut face as another who used Wyatt's saloon as a hang-out.

'This one's name is Miller.' Stanton rose and brushed dust from his right knee. 'Another of Wyatt's hardcases.'

'Does he actually work for Wyatt?'

'He worked for me once, but I soon got rid of him!'

'I guess it's time we talked to Wyatt!' Devlone
said.

'Let's go!' Stanton eased his sixgun in its
holster. 'That four-flusher should be cleaned out.'

They turned and pushed through the gathering
crowd, which followed them as they walked along
the street.

'I want to talk to Wyatt in the first instance,'
said Devlone. 'Just follow my lead, Stanton.'

'You got the deal,' the new sheriff replied
harshly.

Devlone shouldered his way through the
batwings. Pausing on the threshold, he looked
around at the ornate interior. The poker game
was still in progress at the corner table and
Colton was still leaning nonchalantly against the
bar as if he had taken root there. Wyatt was
emerging from his office at the rear of the
building.

Devlone went forward as Wyatt came along the
bar to meet him. The big saloonman began to
smile easily, but there was a snake-like glitter in
his dark eyes. He halted before reaching Devlone,
immaculate as ever, jacket newly pressed and the
collar of his shirt clean and stiff. Devlone felt
dwarfed by Wyatt's size. He noticed that Colton
remained in the background but was watching
intently, like a coiled snake.

'I've been ambushed again, Wyatt,' Devlone
said, his voice crackling in the brooding silence.

'I heard the shooting,' the big man replied
wheezily.

'Ambushed by two of the men who hang out in this place,' Devlone continued. 'Your men, by all accounts.'

'Nothing to do with me!' Wyatt shook his head. 'Just because they use this place for drinking!'

Devlone looked around. There were several hardcases in the big room, apart from the men playing poker, and five others, who had been outside watching Devlone's arrival, were now crowded together on the threshold.

'You better point out the men who work for you,' Devlone said sharply.

'Colton takes care of the hiring and firing,' Wyatt replied.

'Come here, Colton!' Devlone glanced beyond Wyatt's big figure and saw that the gunman was gone from the corner of the bar.

'You want I should fetch him back?' Stanton demanded.

'No!' Devlone shook his head. 'OK, I'm changing the rules now. Stanton, take Wyatt across to the jail and throw him in a cell.'

'You can't do that!' Wyatt's face showed sudden fury. 'I'm a prominent member of this community! I pay my taxes! I do a lot for this county!'

'You'll be running for mayor next!' jeered Stanton. 'Come on, Wyatt, let's go! I've been saving a cell for you ever since I pinned on this law star.'

'Check him for weapons!' Devlone rapped.

'You carrying any hardware?' Stanton demanded.

'What do you want to know, Devlone?' Wyatt shrugged his wide shoulders. 'Sure I employ some of these men!'

Devlone smiled. 'So you are prepared to play ball, huh? OK! Let's talk about Trask and Taylor. They were involved in the shooting that killed Billy Teasdale and put Hank Teasdale on his back. Did they work for you?'

'They rode for me on the range sometimes.'

'So why did they attack the Teasdales? They wouldn't do that unless they were under orders.'

Wyatt shook his head. 'There's been trouble between some of my men and Teasdale's crew, and it must have boiled over the other night.'

'And the two men who just tried to kill me?' Devlone persisted. 'One of them is named Miller! Stanton says he hangs out around here.'

'I know Miller.' Wyatt shrugged. 'He never worked for me.'

'So let's get back to my first question.' Devlone spoke quietly. 'Which of the men present work for you, Wyatt?'

The big saloonman glanced around, pointing out three of the hardcases.

'That's good enough for me!' Devlone turned to survey the big room. 'You men by the door. Step forward those who have jobs.' He paused, waiting for reaction, and he nodded when no one moved. 'None of you have visible means of support! You stand around this place most of the day and night, drinking and gambling, but you don't work. So where do you get your money from?'

The silence intensified, and Devlone glanced at Stanton, whose face was harshly set, his right hand resting on the butt of his holstered gun.

'OK,' Devlone went on. 'I'm serving notice that any man in this town after sundown who doesn't have a job or any visible means of support will be arrested and jailed for vagrancy! Can you make that stick, Stanton?'

'I sure can!' said the new sheriff.

'And you tighten up in here, Wyatt.' Devlone looked into the saloonman's dark eyes. 'One more thing happens which leads to you and you'll see the inside of the town jail. You got that straight?'

'I hear, but you got no trouble coming from my side of the fence. Someone else in this county is pulling the rope.'

Devlone turned and departed, sighing with relief when he stepped out on to the sidewalk. Stanton joined him and they looked around the street.

'You figure you can make that vagrancy thing stick?' Devlone asked.

'I figure I won't have to!' Stanton shook his head. 'Wyatt won't want to lose any of these hardcases. He'll send 'em out to his spread.'

'Follow it up, and go right through the town. Kick out every man with no means of support!' Devlone suppressed a sigh. 'I got another call to make before I can turn in. I'll check with you later at the law office.'

'I'll have the undertaker handle those two stiffs,' Stanton said.

'You're being overworked.' Devlone tried to get his mind working on the broader issues of the case. 'Didn't you say something about getting in a couple of deputies to help?'

'Yeah! But they ain't back from a little trip I sent them on. They'll show up soon, and then things will start buzzing.'

Devlone nodded and turned away. He went back to the hotel, clenching his teeth against the pain in his left leg, and found Rana Teasdale sitting in the lobby. She got to her feet at the sight of him, her eyes wide with shock.

'You don't have anything to fear,' he told her. 'That ambush was for my benefit. But you can't be too careful. Your brother has been killed and your father almost put in his coffin! Someone sure wanted them out of it! Earlier there was talk that your brother was riding with the bunch shooting up the spreads. That might have been the reason for the ambush, because your father made it plain he was gonna take Billy in hand. But I'm not so sure. You said before the shooting that there was friction between your father and Wyatt.'

'There sure was!' The girl's voice filled with anger. 'I was telling you about it when the shooting started. Wyatt wanted to buy the Tall T, and pestered Pa so much he was ordered off the place and told he would be shot if he so much as showed his face there again!'

'Yeah,' Devlone nodded. 'We must get together for another chat soon as I can get round to it.' He touched his hat-brim and turned away.

Leaving the hotel, Devlone went along the alley beside the stable. There was a shack on the back lots and he skirted a heap of trash to reach it. The flimsy wooden door was ajar and he pushed it wide to peer into the gloomy interior, wrinkling his nose at the smell which exuded.

It was a one-room shack with little more than a table and a bunk. A man was sprawled on the bunk, arms outflung, and Devlone frowned. He crossed to the bunk and paused when he saw a large bloodstain on the man's shirtfront! If this was Ira Rosenbloom then he would never tell the law anything about Ballew. He was dead! Devlone turned away.

He walked to the rear of the stable and entered. Bindon was cleaning out one of the stalls, and straightened when Devlone called his name, leaning his broom against a post.

'Glad to see you still in one piece, Ranger!' he observed. 'Heard that shooting and figured someone was trying to put you under.'

'Yeah,' Devlone said. 'You were saying something about Ira Rosenbloom earlier!'

'That's right. But you won't get much sense out of Ira these days!'

'You got any idea what it was he knew about Ballew?'

Bindon grimaced. 'No one paid much attention to Ira. He was allus gabbling about something! But he was drink-sodden and the town gave up on him!'

'He's past all help now!' Devlone observed. 'He's

lying dead in his shack, knifed in the heart. It happened within the last hour, I'd say!'

'Dead!' Bindon turned pale at the news. 'Hell, I saw him staggering down the alley to his shack not more than an hour gone!'

'Have you seen anyone going in the same direction since?'

'Why no! I been pretty busy! Just happened to look out the side window as Ira went by. I ain't seen no one else. Folks don't come down this way unless they got business here in the stable!'

'Do me a favour!' Devlone said. 'Tell Stanton about Rosenbloom!'

He took his warbag and rifle and went back to the hotel, his thoughts churning with conjecture. But there was nothing he could do right now except catch up on some sleep. He went up to his room, locked himself in and checked the window, which overlooked the mainstreet. Then he shaved and generally cleaned up before slumping down on the bed and thankfully closing his eyes....

It was evening before Devlone stirred. He stretched and stifled a yawn, then sat up quickly, instantly alert despite the tiredness still lurking inside him. Getting off the bed, he crossed to the window and peered out. It would be dark in an hour. He buckled on his cartridge belt and tied down the holster, then drew the sixgun and checked it carefully. Opening his warbag, he produced cleaning materials and went through the daily ritual of cleaning and lightly oiling the mechanism of the big weapon before thumbing cartridges into the empty loops on his belt from a box he carried in his bag.

He left the room and locked the door. A void in his stomach warned that he should be filling it with food, and he handed his key to the hotel clerk and went out to the sidewalk, ready for trouble. It seemed that every time he stuck his nose out on the street someone tried to shoot him!

He went to the eating-house and sat at a corner table. A waitress took his order, and while he waited for his meal his thoughts flitted over the salient facts of the case that had evolved since his arrival. There were still a lot of loose ends, but some pointers were slowly evolving. When his food arrived he fell to eating, aware that he could never count on having meals at regular intervals. He ate a well-done beefsteak with all the trimmings and finished up with two cups of strong coffee. Satisfied, he left the eating-house to walk to the jail.

Shadows were crawling into the corners. A strong breeze was blowing along the street, dispersing some of the accumulated heat of the long day, and Devlone studied his surroundings carefully as he moved, looking for suspicious figures and checking out likely ambush spots. He passed Wyatt's saloon and paused to peer in over the batwings, finding the place practically deserted.

Nodding, Devlone continued to the law office and entered to find Stanton sitting behind the desk.

'Have you been off duty since you took over this job from Ballew, Art?' Devlone demanded.

'I've had a couple of sessions of shuteye in one of the cells,' Stanton admitted. 'Did you manage to hit the sack?'

'Yeah. You got the word about Rosenbloom being dead?'

Stanton nodded. 'I checked it out but found no pointers.'

Devlone agreed. 'I asked Wyatt's bartender where Rosenbloom hung out, so they knew I was interested in him.'

'Why did you wanta talk to Ira?'

'I heard he was always saying he knew something bad about Ballew!'

'You figure Ballew might have passed the word for Rosenbloom to cash in?'

'I can't think of a way of proving it! How is Hank Teasdale?'

'Still doing good.'

'Did you get statements from Trask and Taylor about the shooting?'

'Yeah!' Stanton's tone filled with disgust. 'Taylor said he happened to be passing by when it started and he stopped a stray slug! Trask denies any knowledge of what happened. He figures he's innocent.'

'What else you got? Has Ballew changed his story about Snark?'

'Nope. He's still sweating it! But we got to do something about Denning. He's getting mighty restless!'

'What kind of a town marshal was he?'

'He did his job well enough!' Stanton shook his head. 'But there were times when I was hard put to hold myself when I saw him in action. I always got a bad feeling when I was around him!'

'That doesn't make him crooked,' Devlone sighed. 'I respect your gut-feeling, Art, but we need more than that to go on. If we don't have any proof against him then we better turn him loose. But wait till full dark before you do. I'll trail him around for a spell and see what he gets up to.'

'Sounds like a good idea!' Stanton nodded. 'OK, I'll kick him out of here in half an hour.'

'Where is Hank Teasdale being nursed?'

'At the doc's place. He's got a couple of rooms he uses as a hospital.'

'Is there anyone guarding the place?'

'No!' Stanton tensed. 'You figure there could be some more danger for Hank?'

'It would be a good bet to have a guard on hand.' Devlone turned to go. 'I'll be outside waiting for Denning in half an hour.'

'Good luck,' Stanton replied, and Devlone departed....

Darkness was complete when Devlone returned to a vantage point near the jail and concealed himself in the shadows. Chick Denning had been elected to the position of prime mover, and Devlone found a convenient corner and waited patiently for the next development....

EIGHT

Devlone tensed when the law office door was opened and Denning appeared. The ex-town marshal closed the door abruptly and was immediately lost in the surrounding darkness. No sound came from the man, and Devlone squinted his eyes, afraid that Denning suspected what was going on and had ducked silently into the nearest alley. Then a match scraped and flared, illuminating Denning's unshaven face, and the big ex-lawman lit a cigar and stood puffing for several moments while Devlone watched the glowing end of the cigar moving erratically in the shadows. When it moved to the right, Devlone readied himself to follow, intent on keeping Denning's tall figure in view.

Denning passed under a street lantern, his black figure almost invisible when he regained the shadows. Devlone followed on the opposite side of the street, pausing when Denning suddenly crossed the street to the near side. He stepped into the dense shadow of a doorway as the ex-marshal gained the sidewalk only feet from where he was standing.

Dropping back, Devlone followed cautiously, and Denning eventually stopped at the batwings of Wyatt's saloon. Devlone eased forward. For some moments Denning remained motionless, then he shrugged and shouldered his way through the batwings. Devlone went to the nearest window and peered into the brightly lit saloon, narrowing his eyes as he picked out Denning's tall figure in the sparsely populated room.

Denning went along the bar to where Trig Colton was at his usual spot at the far end. There was an animated conversation between the two, and then Colton stepped aside and motioned for Denning to go to Wyatt's office. Devlone watched patiently, saw Denning knock at the door of the office and then enter.

When the door closed behind Denning, Devlone turned to the alley on the right and hurried along it until he reached the side window of Wyatt's office. Approaching cautiously, he dropped to one knee beside the window and peered in at the bottom left-hand corner.

Wyatt was seated at his desk. He was smoking a large cigar and shaking his head slowly when Devlone first set eyes on him. Denning stood before the desk, talking rapidly, but Devlone could not pick up the slightest sound of voices. He tried to lip-read but gave it up as useless and watched intently.

When Denning fell silent, Wyatt asked a question and Denning nodded without hesitation. Wyatt pulled open a drawer in the desk and lifted a box into view, which he opened with a key that was on a chain attached to his belt. He took out a thick wad of notes and carefully counted off a number which he held out to Denning, who leaned forward eagerly and snatched them as if afraid Wyatt would change his mind. Then Wyatt spoke at some length, and Denning put the money into an inside pocket of his broadcloth jacket before turning abruptly to leave the office.

Devlone hurried back to the street and was waiting when Denning came hurrying through the batwings. He eased back into denser shadows, watching patiently, and trailed Denning along the street to the residential part of town. When the ex-lawman paused in front of a white-painted wooden house standing in a quiet location off Main Street, Devlone eased nearer. There were lights in both upper and lower windows of the house. Denning sneaked around to the side, where he was lost to view in dense shadows, and Devlone went forward to gaze at the nameplate on a porch post. Shock stabbed through him when he realized it was the doctor's house!

Devlone moved swiftly, afraid for Hank Teasdale's life. He flattened against the front corner of the house and eased sideways to peer into the shadows where Denning had vanished. Unable to see anything, he listened intently and heard a creaking noise, as if a door was being forced at the rear of the house. He turned immediately and went to the front door.

Grasping the handle, Devlone tried the door,

and to his relief it opened. He entered to find himself in a long, narrow hall. To his left was a flight of stairs, and he mounted swiftly. At the top he approached the nearest door and opened it, to find a darkened bedroom that was unoccupied. Moving fast, he searched the other rooms, finding nothing until he reached a door at the back of the house. A lantern was burning in the room, and when he opened the door he saw Teasdale in a bed and Rana Teasdale seated on a chair beside it.

The girl looked up, her face expressing fear, and Devlone put a finger to his lips, cautioning silence. He closed the door and went to her side.

'We got more trouble,' he warned. 'Sit in that corner and don't move.'

She got silently to her feet and moved her chair.

'I'll be here!' Devlone stood beside a tall wardrobe, concealed from the door. He drew and cocked his sixgun and eased forward until he could cover the door. Silence closed in and he waited, tension clawing at his throat....

Moments later, the door creaked open and Denning appeared, gun in hand. Devlone waited, his sixgun levelled. Denning lifted his Colt and pointed it at Hank Teasdale, and Devlone fired a shot which rocked the room and sent a plume of gunsmoke lancing towards the doorway.

Devlone's bullet hit Denning in the wrist, smashing his hand against the door. The big weapon spilled to the floor from Denning's suddenly nerveless fingers. Blood spurted, and Denning cried out in agony. He reeled sideways against the door, grasping his shattered wrist, and turned to flee. Devlone called to him, and when Denning ignored the warning he stepped forward quickly and crashed the barrel of his gun against the ex-town marshal's head. Denning sprawled to the floor on the landing and lay inert with blood spurting from his wrist.

Devlone bent to check that Denning was out of action, picked up the man's gun and stuck it in the waistband of his pants. He turned and looked into the room. Neither Hank Teasdale nor his daughter had stirred during the incident, but the girl's face was ashen, her eyes wide in shock.

'It's OK now!' he said. 'Just stay put while I attend to the details out here. The danger is over.'

She nodded silently and Devlone stepped outside the room and closed the door. There was a movement on the stairs and he saw the doc's head appearing.

'You're just in time,' Devlone called. 'Denning needs treatment or he'll bleed to death!'

'I'll get my bag!' The doctor turned and hurried back down the stairs, and Devlone checked Denning again. The man was senseless but his hat had saved him from the worst of the blow Devlone had delivered.

There were noises downstairs. Devlone turned to see the doc ascending again, and behind him was a Tall T cowhand. The doc dropped to his knees beside the inert Denning, and Devlone covered the cowboy with his gun until he was sure about him.

'Hank is safe,' he said, 'and I need to get moving. Can you handle Denning when the doc has finished with him? He's to go back to jail.'

'Sure thing,' the cowboy replied. 'Some of my pards are on their way over. They'll be here in a couple of minutes.'

'I wanta see Denning behind bars when I get back to the jail,' Devlone said firmly. 'You got that?'

'You can count on it,' came the firm reply.

'And one of your crew better guard Hank in case there's more trouble.' Devlone turned to the stairs, and as he reached the bottom there was a pounding at the front door. He jerked it open to see three more cowhands.

'Take over here,' he ordered, giving them details of the situation, and left them to it, his mind already occupied with what he had to do. There was a crowd of townsfolk gathering outside, and half a dozen voices clamoured for news. Devlone ignored them. He pushed through their ranks and started along the street....

A burst of gunfire erupted somewhere at the other end of town and Devlone halted in midstride, shocked by the sudden blast of violence. It did not sound like a gun fight, he thought, and began to run in the direction of the disturbance. Several dozen shots were fired in quick succession, and then an uneasy silence settled, leaving echoes that grumbled away into the distance.

Devlone ran along the centre of the street,

pausing in midstride when a single shot blasted
from somewhere ahead. But it was not fired at
him and he continued. He passed Wyatt's saloon
where a couple of men were standing in the light
emanating from its interior, but his attention was
drawn to the street in front of the jail for the
sudden rattle of many hooves warned that
something bad was happening. Then he caught a
glimpse of horses moving fast out of town.

Gaining the sidewalk, Devlone merged with the
shadows, and as he slowed to a walk the sound of
departing hooves died away. Shoulders heaving
he approached the open door of the law office, gun
in hand. The acrid smell of gunsmoke was heavy
and he wrinkled his nose as he hurried into the
building.

The front office was a shambles, filled with
thick gunsmoke drifting towards the open door.
Two dead cowhands lay sprawled on the floor! The
walls of the office were riddled with bullet holes.
The door leading into the cells was open and
Devlone crossed to it, his breathing shallow.
There was a dead silence in the cells – two rows of
cages with a corridor between them, and he
walked along one side, peering into them. Ballew
was on his bunk, dead, blood dripping from
wounds in his chest and head. In another cell
Trask and Taylor were on the floor, also dead. And
three Tall T cowboys were dead in the first cell
opposite, shot where they slept.

Devlone turned when boots pounded the floor of
the office, and Art Stanton appeared in the

connecting doorway, his face frozen in a mask of shock, his mouth gaping slackly in disbelief. He gazed at the bodies in the cells, then came to confront Devlone.

'I heard a shot downtown,' he gasped, 'and figured you were in trouble so I went to take a look. I was the other side of Wyatt's saloon when the shooting here erupted, and when I started back this way someone took a shot at me from cover – the alley beside Wyatt's saloon. I chased him a couple of blocks but lost him, so I came back here.'

Devlone looked around the cell block once more, although the scene was already imprinted on his mind, then moved into the front office, ushering Stanton before him. A couple of townsmen were peering in from the street.

'Fetch the undertaker!' Devlone ordered.

'I am the undertaker!' one replied.

'Then do your job!' Devlone rapped. 'There are half a dozen dead men in here!' He turned to Stanton and told him what had happened when he trailed Denning. 'I figure we ought to pick up Wyatt now!' he ended. 'With him behind bars I reckon most of our problems will end.'

'Yeah! Everything points to Wyatt!' Stanton made a visible effort to pull himself together. 'I'm ready if you are!'

Devlone nodded and drew his gun to check it. He could hear many voices outside, all clamouring for news, and turned to the undertaker, who was staring at the two dead cowhands as if he had never seen a corpse before.

'I want this place clear of bodies by the time we return,' he said.

'Sure!' the undertaker nodded.

'There's plenty of help outside to tote the bodies over to your place.' Devlone looked at Stanton and said, 'OK, let's go to work!'

They departed and walked along the street towards the saloon. More and more townsmen were hurrying towards the jail, and, as they were nearing the saloon, Devlone saw two Tall T cowhands escorting Chick Denning in the same direction and called to them.

'Bring him over here!' he ordered.

Denning was reeling in the grip of the two cowpunchers, eyes half-closed, groaning in pain. His right wrist was heavily bandaged.

'You're in a bad spot, Denning!' Devlone said. He paused but the man made no reply. 'Bring him along with us!' he continued. 'We're gonna have a few words with your boss, Denning, and it might help to have you present.'

He turned to the batwings of the saloon, palming his Colt as he entered. Stanton was at his elbow and the two cowboys brought Denning along, using force to get the big man to do what they wanted. Devlone paused on the threshold and looked around the saloon, which was deserted. The bartender looked up and froze, and Devlone waggled his gun in the man's direction.

'Close up,' he ordered. 'Business is finished for the night.' He started along the bar towards Wyatt's office, but halted when the 'tender spoke.

'Wyatt ain't here now,' the man said. 'He's gone out to his ranch.'

Devlone looked at Stanton. 'Check out this place and make sure it closes. Bring that 'tender along and jail him for the night. I mentioned Rosenbloom to him earlier, and the next minute the man was dead. I'll check at the stable and find out who rode with Wyatt. Then find me a man I can trust to guide me to Wyatt's ranch.'

'You want I should get a posse together?' Stanton said.

'You want to start a war?' Devlone countered. 'Hell, no!'

'OK, if that's the way you want it.' Stanton nodded. 'You'd better be ready for a hot welcome when you ride into Wyatt's place.'

Devlone departed and headed for the stable, where a lantern was burning in the entrance. He slid into the alley beside the barn and approached from the rear, moving silently through the back doorway and walking to the dimly lit office. Hand on his gun and half-expecting a trap, Devlone reached the office and peered inside to see Joe Bindon drowsing at the desk. The ostler was clearly at ease, and Devlone knocked loudly on a post, startling him into wakefulness. Bindon jerked upright, grumbling and rubbing his eyes.

'It's getting so a man can't get a good night's sleep these days!' Bindon muttered, then recognized Devlone. 'So they didn't get you in that shooting!'

'Who were they?' Devlone questioned. 'You must have seen those riders coming in.'

'Yeah, I did! About eight of them! Men you ran out of town earlier because they didn't have a regular job. They made straight for the jail. There was nothing I could do against that number so I watched. They shot the hell out of the place before they rode out again.'

'Did you see any you could put names to?'

'Yeah, a couple. Pete Dunne and Charlie Eke! But Jeb Swanston was on first-name terms with most of them.'

'Jeb Swanston!' Devlone stiffened. 'Hell, I didn't see him in the jail with the others who were gunned down! And he was in one of the cells!'

'You're right! That bunch turned Swanston loose and he came in here before the shooting started. He saddled up the best horse in the place, took his money out of its hiding place, and lit out for points west. I don't figure we're gonna see him back here in many a long day!'

'I'll bring him back if he doesn't leave Texas!' Devlone said harshly. 'And what about Joe Wyatt? He's left town, I'm told!'

'Probably did!' Bindon nodded. 'Cal Fletcher came for Wyatt's rig and Colton's horse about ten minutes before those hardcases rode in.'

'Wyatt doesn't ride a horse?'

'Not any more. Too heavy! He rides a fancy buggy these days!'

'Saddle a horse for me while I fetch my gear.' Devlone turned away. 'Anyone shows up asking for me, tell him to wait until I get back!'

'Sure thing!' Bindon grinned. 'Keep at 'em,

Ranger.'

Devlone hurried to the hotel, collected his gear and then returned to the stable to find two horses standing ready saddled. Bindon appeared from the office followed by a tall, thin man who lifted a hand in greeting.

'Howdy!' he said. 'I'm Dan Gauvin! I'll show you to Wyatt's spread.'

'OK!' Devlone nodded. 'Let's get riding! I'm wasting time.'

They mounted and rode out of town. Gauvin proved to be talkative as they followed a faint trail through the night, and Devlone learned many small facts about the trouble that had come to this range. But time passed, and eventually Gauvin reined in and looked at Devlone.

'This is as far as I go,' he said. 'Over that rise is Wyatt's place.'

'Thanks.' Devlone nodded. 'I can handle it alone from here.'

'I wouldn't wanta be in your boots if you're going after Wyatt alone!' Gauvin shook his head and wheeled his mount around. 'So long!'

Devlone watched until horse and rider vanished in the night then rode on to the top of the rise where he dismounted and dropped into the dust. He bellied forward until he could peer over the skyline. The night was filled with shadows. There was no moon, but enough light came from the stars to enable him to pick out details of his surroundings. The breeze sighed in his ears with nothing but the natural sounds of the night. When he saw a cluster of dark ranch buildings in the middle distance he nodded and got to his feet.

He mounted and rode away from the trail keeping the rise between him and the ranch. Circling right, he aimed for a draw which lay like a black scar in the rising ground and twisted conveniently towards the ranch buildings. When he judged he could get no closer without warning of his presence he dismounted and knee hobbled the horse in thick scrub.

Taking his rifle from the saddleboot, he checked its loads and pocketed a box of cartridges. He moved out and began to circle the ranch on foot, knowing from experience that one determined man might succeed where a posse would only force a fight which might result in many deaths.

He had barely reached the draw when pounding hooves alerted him, coming in fast from the direction of Ash Bend. Taking cover, he lay watching, and soon spotted a rider. He was surprised when there was a noise to his right, and a mounted guard appeared at the top of the draw. He hastily ducked into shadow, and the next instant the newcomer was pulling his horse to a halt only yards away. Then the guard called a harsh challenge.

'Who in hell are you, coming in that fast?'

'Cal Fletcher. I got word for the boss.' The newcomer stopped to speak to the guard. 'Howdy Jack! I got word that the Ranger rode out of town heading in this direction. You gotta be ready for trouble!'

'We're ready!' the guard retorted. 'I heard hooves a few minutes ago but reckoned I was hearing things. Now I ain't so sure. Wyatt's in the house. He offered one hundred bucks for the Ranger! Go talk to him. I'll take a pasear to see if I can raise anything!'

The newcomer rode on to the ranch house, and at that moment the horse that Devlone had tethered in the brush whickered loudly, immediately evoking a reply from the guard's horse. Devlone gritted his teeth, aware that the odds were suddenly stacked against him because the element of surprise was gone. Now they would be ready for him, and he knew what that meant. He had to do this the hard way!

NINE

The guard descended the side of the draw, his
horse slithering on the rough ground, his
attention on the decline, and, as he passed by
Devlone arose and hit him with his rifle butt. The
man pitched sideways out of the saddle and
Devlone grasped the reins as the horse whirled
Soothing the animal, Devlone trailed the reins
and went to the guard, who was unconscious, and
within moments the man was disarmed, gagged
and trussed with his own neckerchief and lariat.

Dumping the unconscious guard in deep brush
Devlone tethered the horse nearby, concerned
that the animal might return to the ranch and
raise the alarm. Then he ascended the incline
until he could look at the ranch. The outlines of
the clustered buildings showed dimly in the night
and he walked in closer. He heard a guard moving
about in the deep shadows on the porch – the clink
of a rifle and the creaking of a loose board as the
man prowled up and down. But he reached the
side of the porch without incident.

Silence pervaded the spread as he moved from

he corner of the house to locate the guard on the porch. He heard the creaking of a rocking chair, and sneaked along the side of the ranch house towards the rear. He was holding his rifle, and looked around for a spot where he could leave it handy in case it was needed urgently. He bent and placed it on the ground beside the rear corner of the building, but, as he straightened, a sudden glimpse of movement on the corner alerted him, and the next instant a burly figure cannoned into him. There was a harsh curse, and then a voice spoke in a hoarse undertone.

'Hell, Mike, I didn't hear you! What in hell's going on? Who was on the hoss that came into the front yard?'

'Cal Fletcher,' Devlone replied. 'He brought word that the Ranger is on his way here.'

'Then we better be on our toes. I could sure do with a hundred bucks for killing that sonofabitch!' The figure paused. 'Hey, you ain't Mike Farrant!'

Devlone reacted instinctively, his sixgun clearing leather even as the man spoke. He stepped in close, swinging the big gun, and laid the muzzle against the side of the guard's head. The man gasped and slumped, and Devlone caught and lowered him to the ground. Taking the man's gun, Devlone stuck it into his waistband. Then he grasped the man and dragged him away from the house into deep shadow. He removed the man's gunbelt, took the pants belt and bound his wrists with it, then used the gunbelt to bind his legs together. Finally, he removed the dusty neckerchief and gagged the man with it.

Within moments he was back at the rear of the house, but saw nothing to alarm him, and tried the back door of the house. It was bolted on the inside. He moved to the kitchen window but again was unlucky. It was securely fastened.

Passing to the other side of the house, he made his way to the porch and peered around the front corner. He could still hear a regular creaking sound as the guard teetered to and fro on the rocking chair.

'Hey, Mike!' Devlone called in an undertone. 'What's going on out front? Who rode in?'

The guard came to the side of the porch towering over Devlone. It was so dark Devlone could have carved his initials on the shadows.

'You getting nervous?' The guard explained the news he had received from Cal Fletcher. 'So we gotta be ready for anything! You better get round the back again. Wyatt'll have your guts if you don't do your job properly!'

Devlone reached up a big hand to grasp the back of the guard's gunbelt as the man glanced towards the gate, and jerked with all his strength, pulling him over the rail and striking with his sixgun before the body could hit the ground. The man relaxed instantly.

Devlone dragged him away from the house and hog-tied him, then returned to the porch and walked to the front door. Gun in hand, he opened the door and entered, pausing only to bolt the door. There was lantern light inside. Devlone blinked, looking around the narrow entrance lobby, noting three doors opening off it on his right and two on the left. Light showed under two of the doors on his right and he went to the nearest, thrust it open and levelled his Colt. A big man was seated at a desk in the room. He looked around at Devlone and sprang up in alarm, reaching for the butt of his holstered gun.

'Hold it!' Devlone rapped, but the man continued. Devlone lifted his thumb from his hammer and the weapon blasted, throwing a slug into the man's chest. The shock of the shot struck through the room as the man fell down beside the desk, blood spurting from a half-inch hole bored through his ribs. Devlone turned away, making for the second door.

He was reaching out to grasp the handle when the door was pulled open from inside and a man appeared, sixshooter in hand. Devlone sidestepped and struck quickly with his Colt, hoping to bust the man's wrist, but a shot was squeezed off even as the muzzle of his gun smashed against the man's gun arm. The bullet crackled in Devlone's ear on its blind flight into the opposite wall.

Devlone struck again, this time at the man's head, and caught the body as it pitched to the floor. Holding the man, he kicked open the door, and a gun inside the room blasted twice in quick succession, one bullet breathing on Devlone and the other taking the man he held through the chest. There was a figure across the room, wreathed in gunsmoke, and Devlone fired then moved on to check the other rooms.

As he thrust open the third door on his right Devlone heard a door behind him being pulled open. He swung around as a man appeared in the doorway opposite, gun lifting, and Devlone fired yet again, his bullet downing the man. Going forward, he peered into the room from around the doorpost and saw Joe Wyatt standing behind a desk, holding a gun.

The saloonman fired instantly, his bullet clipping the doorpost. Devlone took an extra moment to aim before firing in return and his slug hit Wyatt in the right shoulder. The big man threw down his gun, stumbled backwards, then dropped to his knees, his left hand lifting to press against a spurt of blood from his wound. His face was haggard, his mouth gaping in shock.

Devlone entered the room and kicked the door shut behind him. The black muzzle of his Colt gaped at Wyatt, who remained on his knees as if in prayer.

'Resisting arrest!' Devlone said. 'That'll hold you while I sort out the crookedness in this county.'

'Are you loco?' Wyatt demanded. 'You came busting into my house and opened fire without warning.'

'Save it, Wyatt. I got enough on you. There are witnesses. You're finished, mister! There'll be a necktie party after your trial, and you'll be the main event.'

'You expect to get me out of here and back to

ail?' Wyatt grinned despite his pain. 'I got a dozen ough gunmen who won't hesitate to kill you.'

'And I got a posse round the place, just waiting o shoot the hell out of it!' Devlone bluffed. He olted the door and moved towards Wyatt, kicking he man's discarded gun into a corner. 'On your eet, mister.'

He reloaded his gun as Wyatt struggled to his eet. The man's heavy face was contorted. He lumped into a seat, glaring at Devlone.

'So what happens now?' he demanded. 'I can't valk! Do you reckon to carry me out of here?' He aughed hoarsely, breath wheezing in his massive hest.

'I got plenty of time,' Devlone shrugged. 'I'll sit ight till dawn, when the posse will come in. How ong do you figure your crew will hang around?'

'You're bluffing! You couldn't have got a posse ogether in the time! You came out here alone in he hope of picking me off!'

'Which I've done!' Devlone moved into a corner vhere he could watch the window and the door, oulling a chair into a position where he would be overed from the window by Wyatt's massive igure. He sat down. 'Time is on my side.'

'I'm bleeding badly!' Wyatt stifled a groan. 'I need the doc!'

'That's too bad! You'll have to wait until the chance to leave comes up.'

Wyatt groaned. 'I'll bleed to death before norning,' he gasped.

'Shut up!' Devlone had heard a sound outside

the door, and as silence came he heard it again
Someone was trying the door. He saw the handle
move.

'Hey, boss, are you in there?' a voice demanded
'Lowery is dead and so are Kenton and Moss!
checked outside and the guards have gone!'

'Stand away from that door,' Devlone replied
loudly. 'Wyatt is in here, wounded and under
arrest. A posse will be riding in around dawn, and
anyone still on the ranch at that time will be
arrested and thrown in the jail in Ash Bend.'

There was no reply from outside, and Devlone
grinned at Wyatt.

'Come sun-up there won't be a man on the
spread apart from the two of us,' he said. 'You'll
get no help from hired hands when the chips are
down.'

'I'm bleeding badly,' Wyatt said harshly. 'You
better do something about it or you'll have a
corpse on your hands come sun-up.'

Devlone holstered his gun and went to the
saloonman's side, checking the bullet wound in
the big man's shoulder.

'It ain't too bad,' he judged. 'I reckon you might
not get the full use of the shoulder back, but it'l
heal, and time is the one thing you've got plenty
of. Think on that while we wait for the posse
There's been murder and bad things done around
the county, and you're elected to shoulder the
blame.'

'You can't pin any of that on me!' Wyatt
groaned. 'OK! I grabbed a few acres of rangeland

ut I never had a hand in the robberies or urders. You got to look elsewhere for the men sponsible, and you only need one name. Ballew! knew it a long time ago, but it suited my purpose keep my mouth shut. What Ballew and his ooked crew were doing covered up my own ctivities so I left him alone.'

Devlone considered the saloonman's words, aaking his head as he tried to get a complete cture in his mind.

'I figured Ballew was working with you,' he id. 'And Denning! I saw you give money to enning, and then he went out to kill Hank easdale.'

'I didn't want anyone killed!' Wyatt shook his ead. 'All I wanted was to force the ranchers to ll out. And I was willing to pay a fair price.'

Devlone kept his ears strained as he listened to yatt, certain the gunmen at the door would tempt to get into the room. Tension pressed in ound him, and he suddenly stiffened, drawing s sixgun as he snapped at Wyatt.

'Shut up and listen!'

The saloonman fell silent as Devlone eased back to his corner. A faint scratching sound was ming from the heavily curtained window.

'If there's shooting and you move an inch in that at I'll gutshoot you!' Devlone warned. 'Just pray at none of your men mistake you for me.'

'This ain't the way to handle the law!'

'That ain't the way I see it!' Devlone retorted. ve got to stay alive so I can do my job.'

'There's only one way out for you,' Wyatt snarled, 'and that's feet first.'

Devlone aimed for the top right-hand corner of the window and triggered a shot which shattered the glass. As the echoes faded a gun outside returned fire, and Devlone ducked behind Wyatt's big figure as bullets blasted across the room. Gunsmoke caught at Devlone's throat as he prepared to fight. But the grim echoes faded and full silence returned. He looked at Wyatt hunched in his seat, and the saloonman glowered at him.

'Like I said,' Devlone observed. 'I got all night!'

A hand suddenly appeared at the window grasping the curtains and tugging at them. Devlone fired and the hand jerked away, accompanied by a screech of pain, but the curtains were dragged from the window, leaving a bare aperture with broken glass and the dark night pressing in blankly from outside. Devlone kept low, ensuring that Wyatt's figure masked him. He left the lamp alight because he needed to see.

'You're for it now!' snarled Wyatt.

'I got nothing to lose!'

'They're gonna pick you off from out there!'

'You're twice my size,' Devlone countered. 'They'll have to shoot through you to hit me!'

'Hey, you in the house!' a harsh voice called from outside the window. 'Throw down your gun and come on out. If we have to come in after you we'll bury you in the morning.'

'You better start thinking about your getaway.

Devlone replied. 'There's a posse following me from town, and Wyatt is shot bad and like to bleed to death before morning, so you ain't doing him any favours by trying to get me.'

'Is that so, boss?' the voice demanded.

'Yeah! I'm bad hurt!' Wyatt said. 'And the Ranger is using me as a shield. You can't hit him from the window without nailing me!'

'I couldn't have put it better myself,' Devlone said.

He heard voices outside the window, but they were not loud enough for him to make out what was being said, and he guessed the hardcases were about to try something else. He eased slightly to his left to make the angles to his position more acute. Thumbing fresh cartridges into his gun, he hunched his big shoulders.

Moments later there was a heavy crash at the door, which splintered and shook. Devlone eased down beside Wyatt. A gun crashed at the window and the bullet breathed on Devlone's neck in passing. He returned a shot at the window, then fired three spaced shots into the door, hearing a screech of agony as one of them found flesh outside. The gun at the window kept hammering, and gunsmoke drifted through the room.

Devlone saw a gun at the window and triggered two shots, then swung his attention to the door as shots were fired through it. Wyatt slid to the floor, and Devlone was forced to go down because he was exposed to the window. A bullet tugged at his hatbrim and he sent a shot at the window, then two more through the door. The shooting tailed off then and he reloaded.

'You're a damn fool, Ranger!' Wyatt said raggedly.

Devlone wrinkled his nose at the reek of gunsmoke. There was a sting in his right cheek and he felt blood there. A bullet had nicked him! He watched both door and window, reflexes hair-triggered. Wyatt was lying on the floor, and grinned tightly when Devlone met his gaze.

'I'm waiting to see you get it, Ranger! You know you ain't gonna get out of here alive!'

'Hey, boss!' a voice called from outside the door. 'You want us to come in and get you?'

'Anyone comes through that door and Wyatt collects a slug,' Devlone said.

'He's bluffing, Jake,' Wyatt shouted. 'He won't shoot me in cold blood.'

A gun blasted at the window, and more shots were fired through the door. Devlone held his fire, waiting for a definite target. The door was struck several times by a heavy object and splintered still more. Devlone fired through it, spacing his shots waist high, then ducked and reloaded again.

The door finally gave way and fell apart. Devlone was ready, and started shooting as soon as he saw an indistinct figure beyond the door. A man yelled hoarsely and fell forward, sprawling through the doorway while still trying to level his gun at Devlone, who fired again and sent a heavy slug smacking into the man's forehead. A gun at the window hammered rapidly, and Wyatt yelled as one of the slugs creased his thick shoulder.

'Hold off!' he shouted. 'You fools are hitting me!'

'We're doing the best we can, boss,' someone replied.

'Your time is running out!' Devlone called. 'Leave now or you'll lose the chance. That posse should be riding in at any time.' He grinned at Wyatt. 'I told you I got this tied down, Wyatt!'

Silence closed in and Devlone maintained his grim vigil, gun ready for action. Gunsmoke was thick in the room, and rasped at the back of his throat. He looked at Wyatt, although his concentration did not waver. The saloonman was pale, his eyes feverishly bright.

'Most of your crew will have lit out by now.' Devlone observed. 'Mebbe they got some sense after all!'

'Why don't you stick your nose out the window to find out?'

Devlone returned his attention to the window, and the next instant a flaming brand was hurled into the room. Wyatt lumbered upright, cursing. Devlone reached out a long arm, grasped the saloonman's leg and heaved with all his strength. Wyatt crashed to the floor, and must have fallen on his wounded shoulder for he groaned and relaxed.

'You coming out now, Ranger?' someone yelled.

Devlone looked at the burning brand. Fire was already taking hold of the tinder-dry floorboards. He looked at Wyatt, saw that the man was unconscious, and thumbed a shot at the lamp across the room. The slug smashed the lamp and overturned it, and Devlone gritted his teeth when he saw it crash to the floor and add to the growing conflagration.

A burst of shooting erupted from the doorway. Long red tongues of muzzle flame speared amidst the billowing smoke. A bullet creased Devlone's left forearm and he triggered his gun rapidly, ears protesting at the explosions. A gun joined in at the window and he canted his muzzle and bracketed it before swinging back to cover the door. Inside the room, flames spread surprisingly quickly, flickering voraciously, and heat seared Devlone's face.

It was time to get out, he thought, pushing himself to one knee. The window was clear now, but shots still hammered into the room through the open doorway. Devlone looked at Wyatt's motionless figure and shook his head. He could not leave the saloonman to burn! Reloading his gun, he surged upright and launched himself at the window, hunching his shoulders as his feet left the ground. He dived forward at the window aperture, thankful the shooting had broken the glass. His hat took the brunt of his impact with the window frame and he sailed through and fell heavily onto the ground outside, aware that at least two guns started shooting at him almost before he landed.

Rolling swiftly, he came up firing, aiming for the bright flashes confronting him. A bullet nicked his left ear and he rolled to the left, returned to a firing position and resumed shooting. Gun echoes resounded in the distance, and Devlone sprang to his feet and hurled himself away from the house, gun still ready for action. He ran three swift paces before dropping to the ground, and now there was no one shooting at him.

He reloaded, ears singing from the shock of the gunshots. Looking towards the house, he saw flames leaping up in the room he had vacated, and knew he had to go back inside to get Wyatt. He pushed himself up and moved fast to the front corner of the house, twice stumbling over sprawled bodies lying in the darkness.

Reaching the front door, he lunged inside. A figure moved and he fired. A gun flashed in reply, but the muzzle was pointing at the floor, triggered by a nerveless hand as his target pitched forward in death.

Devlone went into Wyatt's room and paused on the threshold. The saloonman was hunched on the floor, and Devlone went to his side, lifting his left arm to shield his face from the flames. He holstered his gun and bent to take hold of Wyatt's shoulders to drag the man from the room. But as he reached the door and comparative safety, Wyatt came to life unexpectedly, his right fist crashing against Devlone's jaw. The blow took Devlone unawares and he toppled backwards. Shaking his head, he rolled as the saloonman came at him in a desperate attempt to follow up his advantage.

Wyatt lumbered forward as Devlone got up, but unable to make it, Devlone dropped on to his back and kicked upwards with both feet, shoulder thrusting against the floor for extra purchase. Wyatt ran into the feet, and Devlone stiffened his legs, his knees bending as he took the weight. He feared the man would plunge on top of him but thrust with all his might and Wyatt was flung backwards.

Devlone surged upright, palming his gun. He went through the doorway after Wyatt, who had cannoned into the wall opposite and was sliding to the floor. Halting quickly, Devlone stood with ready gun, still determined to end the action or die in the attempt. He drew a deep breath as he gazed at the motionless saloonman, and realized that for the moment it was over....

TEN

Devlone dragged Wyatt out of the house and dumped him on the porch. The cool night breeze hit him in the face as he straightened. With gun poised for action, he peered into the shadows, looking for more trouble, but the night was quiet now and he figured Wyatt's crew had finally pulled out. He checked the loads of his gun before holstering the weapon, then bound Wyatt's wrists together and went to check inside the house.

The fire had taken furious hold, rapidly engulfing the woodwork, and Devlone dragged out the bodies of the men he had killed. There were two dead men outside by the window and he toted them to the front of the house, where they made a grim line in the yard. Fetching his rifle from where he had left it, he brought in the two guards he had captured. Flames were now leaping through the windows and spreading to the roof, fanned by a strong breeze.

Devlone searched the rest of the ranch and found it deserted. There were signs of frenzied departure in the bunkhouse. He went to the barn and harnessed a grey to the buggy within, then took the vehicle over to the house and put Wyatt and the two guards in it. Wyatt was conscious now, but remained silent as Devlone manhandled him into the buggy.

Devlone felt easier when he was in his saddle and heading for the distant town, leading the buggy and ignoring Wyatt's complaints as the vehicle rattled and lurched over the rough trail. The two trussed guards remained silent....

A rifle cracked in the shadows and a bullet clipped Devlone's hat-brim. He tugged his rifle from its boot as he dived from his saddle. His horse stopped immediately, and the buggy halted. Echoes faded across the darkened range. Regaining his feet, Devlone kept close to the buggy and peered around.

'I knew my outfit wouldn't hightail it!' Wyatt laughed. 'Now you're in trouble, Ranger. They let you clear the house to get you in the open.'

Devlone looked around, ears strained for sounds of hooves. He went back to his mount and swung into the saddle.

'The best thing you can do, Ranger,' Wyatt jeered, 'is hightail it. Trig Colton will be back soon, and if you're still around he'll bury you!'

Trig Colton! Devlone gripped his rifle and peered around into the darkness. Under the pressure of law business he had forgotten about the gunman!

'That stopped you in your tracks!' Wyatt observed. 'Figured you'd busted us wide open and nailed us down, huh? Well ain't you due for a shock! You won't get me to town! The play ain't finished yet, not by a long rope.'

Devlone went to his horse, swung into the saddle and continued, leading the grey. He looked around constantly. The sky was lightening to the east and he realized that if he was still on the trail at sun-up he would make an easy target for backshooters. He pushed on faster, ignoring Wyatt's harsh voice.

Another shot crackled through the dawn, and once more he dived from the saddle. He noted the position of the flash but would not be drawn away from his prisoners. He resumed riding, aware that the situation would change in his favour when the sun came up....

Twice more Devlone was forced to dismount by flying lead, but each time he regained his saddle and pushed on. Wyatt had fallen into an uneasy silence, and, as they continued, dawn crept imperceptibly into the sky. Devlone watched his surroundings intently as the gloom was slowly relieved. Soon there was a faint tinge of red to the east, and objects around him began to appear as the sun approached.

Gaunt-faced and tired, Devlone looked around intently when full daylight came. He was carrying his Winchester, the barrel resting across his saddlehorn. The sun came up, throwing red-gold fingers of brilliance across the bleak range. Heat began to permeate, and Devlone eased himself in the jolting saddle, weary beyond belief.

An hour later Ash Bend appeared in the distance and Devlone urged the grey to greate effort. Wyatt and the other two prisoners had been silent since dawn, and he checked them. Wyatt was unconscious or asleep, his head lolling sideways, a great stain of blood on his shirt at the right shoulder. The other prisoners were awake, morosely silent as the reality of jail loomed larger with each passing minute.

Devlone twisted in the saddle to check his back trail and stiffened at the sight of two distant figures spurring along behind, gaining on him with each passing moment. His eyes frosted as he checked his rifle and looked once more towards the town to gauge the distance. He urged the horses into a trot and the buggy jolted along, wheels grating in the ruts of the trail.

They reached the outskirts of town still well ahead of the two riders, and Devlone sighed with relief as he halted the rig in front of the law office. Ash Bend was slowly coming awake.

The door of the law office opened as Devlone dismounted and Art Stanton appeared, haggard of face and hard-eyed. He stared at Devlone as if seeing a ghost, and shook his head when he saw the three prisoners in the buggy.

'Looks like you had the helluva night!' he observed.

'And then some!' Devlone looked around. 'Let's get these three behind bars and I'll tell you what happened.'

Wyatt cursed as he was dragged out of the

buggy, and Stanton led him into the office while Devlone brought along the other two. When the prisoners were behind bars, Devlone took the opportunity to relax, and filled Stanton in on what had happened at Wyatt's ranch.

'There's no doubt about Wyatt's guilt!' Stanton observed. 'I'll get a statement from him and the other two.'

'There are still some loose ends that need tying,' Devlone said wearily. 'But they ain't so urgent. You got the town tied down now, huh?'

'You can bet your life on it!' Stanton's face was grim. 'Nothing can move around this burg without me getting to hear about it. The way Ballew and Denning ran things, there was no respect for the law. But we've changed that!'

'Someone was taking shots at me all the way to town, and as I came in two riders were on my back trail. I didn't see hide nor hair of Trig Colton out there. See what you can learn about him from Wyatt and the other two.'

'If he's still around we'll get him,' Stanton said firmly.

Devlone was not so sure as he left the office and swung wearily into his saddle. He reined about to ride to the livery barn, the clip of his hooves sounding loud in the silence of the early morning.

Dismounting in the stable yard, he let the horse drink from the trough before leading it into the barn, and when he stepped into the wide doorway of the dusty building a gun blasted almost in his face, the bullet ripping through the crown of his

Stetson as orange muzzle flame plumed towards
him.

Devlone reacted without thought, hurling
himself down and reaching for his gun, and such
was his speed the big Colt was in his right hand
and ready for action as he hit the ground. He
caught a glimpse of a man in the gloomy interior
of the nearest stall, wreathed in gunsmoke and in
the act of taking fresh aim. He thumbed off a shot
which shook the wooden building and the man
twisted and fell heavily.

Breathing hard, Devlone looked around
quickly, recalling the two riders he had seen on
his back trail. He rolled into the cover of the stall
opposite, then got to one knee, gun upraised. His
ears were ringing from the crash of the shooting
and the acrid stench of gunsmoke reeked in his
nostrils. Gaining his feet, he walked through the
stable to the rear door and peered outside. Two
saddle horses were standing with trailing reins in
the corral, and Devlone clenched his teeth as he
looked around for the second man.

There was a faint sound to Devlone's rear and
he whirled, his gun swinging to cover the figure
coming towards him, his finger trembling on the
trigger, but he lowered the weapon, recognizing
Jake Bindon, the ostler.

'I might have guessed it was you!' Bindon
rubbed his eyes. 'A man cain't sleep peacefully
around here no more!'

'You just might be able to after today!' Devlone
retorted. 'Take a look at the horses out back and

ell me who rides them.'

Bindon went to the door. 'That bay is Trig Colton's horse,' he said.

Devlone nodded, and checked his gun before holstering it. 'Now take a look at the man I just killed up front,' he said grimly.

They walked to the front stall and Bindon bent over the prostrate figure sprawled in the straw. His eyes were wide with shock when he faced Devlone.

'It's Sam Wenn, one of Wyatt's hardcases.' he reported.

Devlone walked into the yard, and saw a rider coming in from the trail, riding fast, a sure sign that trouble had struck somewhere.

'Who's that?' he demanded, and Bindon shaded his eyes.

'Pete Riley, one of Teasdale's crew, and he's hurt, by the looks of him!'

Devlone had already noted that the rider was swaying in his saddle, and as the man came into the yard it was easy to see blood on his shirtfront. He went out to meet the rider, who reined up and slid out of the saddle, hanging on to the saddlehorn for support. His face was grey with shock and he seemed barely conscious.

'There's been hell to pay at the Tall T,' he reported. 'There was only me and Tom Bender on the spread when Colton and Wenn showed up. They killed Bender and left me for dead, then fired the place. When they left I got out of the bunkhouse as it burned down, and came on here quick as I could.'

Footsteps sounded nearby and Devlone looke
round to see Stanton running towards them, gu
in hand.

'Colton is loose in town,' he rapped as Stanto
reached them, 'and I figure he's come in to ki
Teasdale. We better get to the doc's place pronto!'

Stanton whirled instantly, and Devlone had t
half-run to keep up with him as they crossed th
yard and started along the street.

'I got a man on guard at the doc's afte
Denning's attempt to kill Hank last evening
Stanton reported.

'That was good thinking!' Devlone was soo
breathless. 'We better separate some. Trig Colto
is mighty fast with a gun!'

'You ain't no slouch yourself!' Stanton retorted.

A gun blasted in the early morning, the soun
coming from the direction in which they wer
running. Devlone drew his sixgun and checked i
as he continued, then eased out to the centre o
the street while Stanton remained close to th
sidewalk. From his open position, Devlone had a
better angle on the buildings ahead, and was soo
able to see the front of the doc's house. The echoe
of the shot were still growling away into th
distance.

Slowing to a walk, Devlone heard a hoarse voic
calling from an upper window of the house the
were making for.

'Stanton, this is Ike Benton! I just scared of
Trig Colton! He was trying to bust in the bac
door and I put a slug through it. He took off, and

me up front and saw him disappear into the
ley opposite.'

Devlone spun and covered the alley, then moved
ross the street to check it out. It was deserted,
d he turned as Stanton came to his side.

'Wyatt's bunch sure mean to wipe out
easdale's crew,' Stanton observed.

'And send Teasdale to join his son!' Devlone's
ice was harsh. 'What's Colton likely to do now?'

'Wyatt's saloon?' Eagerness showed in Stan-
n's face.

Devlone nodded. 'That's what I figure! Come
!'

'I put a couple of men in the saloon last night to
rest any of Wyatt's bunch that showed up,'
anton said.

'You ain't been missing any shots!' Devlone
oved back along the street.

'We get Colton and there won't be any others to
und up,' Stanton said. 'I figure he's the last of
yatt's crooked bunch.'

They reached the front of the saloon and
evlone peered in over the batwings, narrowing
s eyes against the shadows inside.

'Watch out for my men,' Stanton warned.
hey're liable to shoot first and ask questions
terwards!' He came to Devlone's side and called
udly. 'Hey, Clayton, Jack Belmont! You in
ere? This is Art Stanton!'

There was no reply. The big room was deserted,
d Devlone thrust himself through the batwings
d moved to the right to place his back to a wall.

Stanton entered quickly and slid to the left into
similar position.

'Where in hell are Clayton and Belmont
Stanton complained. 'I gave them a stri
warning. If they took advantage of the situatio
and drank themselves stupid I'd roast them over
branding fire!'

Devlone was watching the silent room, his b
sixgun poised in his right hand. 'It looks like w
got to do this the hard way,' he said.

'Yeah! Go through the place room by room
Stanton nodded.

'You got it!' Devlone moved forward. 'Cover me

Stanton lifted his long-barrelled Colt an
crouched a little. Devlone crossed to the long ba
and looked behind it, finding nothing. He turne
to check out the lower rooms of the saloon, an
paused when Colton appeared in the doorway
Wyatt's office, ominous in black clothes, his rigl
hand down at his side holding his Colt, the muzz
pointing at the saw-dusted floor.

'I got you dead to rights, Ranger!' Colto
snapped. 'Drop your gun! I can kill you before yo
move a muscle!'

Stanton was out of Colton's vision and swun
his gun quickly, the movement attracting Colto
who half-turned to cover Stanton. Devlone move
at the same time, his gun lifting, and he fired
split second before Colton could work his gun. Th
blast of Colt-fire rocked the building. Devlone wa
the first to fire, and his muzzle was gaping a
Colton's chest as the bullet was discharge

Colton took the impact of the flying chunk of lead before he could get into action, the bullet smashing his breast-bone and slamming into his heart. He unhinged at the knees, waist and neck, his gun spilling from a suddenly nerveless hand, and he was dead before he hit the floor.

Devlone remained stock-still, ears protesting against the shock of the shot, his nostrils flaring. He watched the fallen body for signs of further resistance although he knew Colton was dead. Echoes faded, and Stanton came to Devlone's side, holstering his gun.

'You must be twice as fast as Colton was,' Stanton observed. 'I saw him in action once down Val Verde way, and he was faster than chain lighting.'

'There's always someone faster,' Devlone said quietly, breaking his stance. 'We better find your two men!'

They went through the building, and when Devlone kicked open the door of Wyatt's office he saw two men on the floor. One was in the act of getting to his feet. The other was unconscious, with blood on his face.

'Colton's in the saloon!' the man gasped when he saw Stanton.

'Who's Colton?' demanded Stanton, and Devlone felt tensions suddenly ooze out of his big frame. He holstered his gun and gave vent to a long sigh.

'I guess it's time to start putting the pieces together,' he said softly. 'But before that there's something important I have to do.'

'What's that?' Stanton demanded.

'Get some breakfast!' Devlone smiled.

'Do you figure we got the bits and pieces settled?'

'Yeah! The whole truth will come out now.' Devlone nodded. 'There's only one loose end needs tying, but that can wait. What you need to do is get statements from the prisoners. They'll soon start talking one against the other.'

'The eating-house is along there!' Stanton pointed the way. 'The county owes you a vote of thanks, Devlone. You sure didn't let the grass grow under your feet!'

Devlone smiled and went looking for the eating-house, relaxing for the first time since his arrival. He heard a rider coming along the street from behind and, out of habit, turned to check him out, his eyes widening as he took in details. The man was tall, like a scarecrow! The horse was brown, with a white left foreleg!

Alertness surged through Devlone. Snark's killer! Details of the ambusher's appearance were etched into Devlone's mind, and he realized he was looking at the man in the flesh! He saw the killer stop and speak to Stanton, who was standing on the edge of the sidewalk. They seemed friendly, more than mere acquaintances, Devlone noted with professional interest. The ambusher dismounted and trailed his reins, apparently ready to do more than pass the time of day with the new sheriff.

Devlone's first instinct was to go back along the

dewalk,and his right hand eased the sixgun in
is holster. He saw the ambusher glance around,
nd the man's eyes narrowed as he met Devlone's
aze. Then he relaxed. But Devlone saw the man's
unhand drop to his holstered weapon and remain
1ere.

Devlone paused, suspicion overwhelming his
1ind, and, as he continued on his way to the
ating-house, his thoughts were racing. He
lanced back at Stanton and the ambusher and
aw them still talking animatedly, heads
)gether, but the ambusher was looking in
)evlone's direction, and Devlone entered the
ating-house, determined to fill his stomach
efore attempting to settle the one incident he
ad not yet had the opportunity to handle.

He ate his fill as dark reflection cluttered his
1ind. Art Stanton had seemed rigidly honest in
ll his actions! But he had conveniently left the
ail when the killers struck and killed all those
1en, and he was on more than casual terms with
he bushwhacker who had killed Snark. He
urned the situation over in his mind, aware that
omehow he had to test the new sheriff. He was
rinking his second cup of coffee when the street
.oor opened and Stanton entered, followed closely
y the ambusher, and Devlone's expression
emained unchanged as they approached his
able.

Stanton was smiling easily, his manner normal.
Iowdy, Devlone,' he greeted. 'I guess it's time for
reakfast! This will be one hell of a busy day, but

first things first, huh?' He glanced at his silent
companion, who was gazing at Devlone with the
impersonal gaze of a rattlesnake. 'This is Ma
Jackson. He works for me. I've been waiting for
him to get back from a job he was doing over
Malpasa way. He's a good man in a fight! May we
sit down?'

'Sure!' Devlone smiled. 'Howdy, Jackson! How
you doing?' He arose as Stanton sat down, and for
a moment it seemed that Jackson was going to
push the issue then and there. But the man
nodded an acknowledgement and sat down as
Devlone turned to the door. 'I'll drop by the office
later,' Devlone said, holding Stanton's gaze. 'We'll
get statements from the prisoners.'

'No sweat!' Stanton nodded. 'I figure we got the
town hog-tied now!'

Devlone went out to the street. Jackson's horse
was at the hitch-rail and he went to the animal
took a Winchester from its saddle scabbard and
ejected a 30-30 cartridge into the dust. Returning
the weapon to its boot, he picked up the cartridge
and examined it to find two scratches on the
bright metal. This was the weapon that had fired
the fatal slug at Snark!

He went along the street to the gunsmith's
shop. Ike Carson was sweeping the sidewalk out
front. Producing the cartridge he had removed
from Jackson's Winchester, Devlone handed it to
the gunsmith.

'Check this against the shell case I gave you and
tell me if they came from the same weapon,' he said

Carson led the way into his shop, examining the
cartridge. He opened a small drawer and took out
the empty case Devlone had brought in pre-
viously, using a magnifying glass to compare the
scratches. When he looked up at Devlone there
was certainty on his seamed face.

'The same ejector made the scratches on both
cartridges,' he said firmly.

Devlone nodded. 'That's what I figured! Keep
those cartridges until I produce the gun that made
those scratches. Then you can do some tests on it.'

'Certainly! Whose gun is this?'

'That doesn't matter. I'll come back to you later.'

Devlone departed and stood on the sidewalk
thinking about the situation. Suspicion was still
rife in his mind and he needed to consider it. He
walked back to the eating-house and entered the
alley at the side to look through a window.
Stanton and Jackson were still there. The pair
were almost through eating, and he waited,
reluctant to tackle Jackson in a public place. He
thought over his investigation. Nothing had been
overlooked. With the arrest of Snark's killer the
case would end naturally....

Stanton arose and started for the door with
Jackson following. When they left the eating-
house Devlone watched from cover, and was
satisfied when they walked towards the law office,
Jackson leading his horse. Devlone followed at a
distance. Jackson tied his horse to the hitchrail,
and Devlone quickened his stride when they
disappeared into the law building.

Devlone took Jackson's rifle from its saddle bo
and ejected its loads, letting the bright cartridg
fall into the dust. He worked the mechanis
heavy-handedly, and on the fifty movement t
ejector failed, jamming the weapon as t
gunsmith had foretold. Devlone went to the do
of the office and entered, carrying the useless ri
in his left hand. Stanton was sitting at his des
Jackson was leaning against the door that led in
the cell block. With his hand close to the butt
his holstered sixgun, Devlone closed the door wi
his right heel and walked to the desk, keepi
Jackson under observation although it seem
that his attention was on Stanton. He sa
Jackson stiffen and ease his gunhand towards t
butt of his holstered sixgun.

'I'm sorry you're hankering on pulling out fro
this range,' Stanton was saying to Jackso
'You've worked for me a long time, Mal.'

'I figure it's time for a change,' Jackson growle

'Howdy.' Devlone spoke casually. He hefted t.
Winchester. 'This is the weapon that closes n
case.' He saw Stanton frown, and smiled, turni
his full attention to Jackson. 'Catch!' He toss
the weapon to the man and Jackson caught
instinctively. Devlone moved to the side of t
desk where it would be difficult for Stanton to li
up a gun on him. 'Snark was killed by
ambusher when I had him under arrest. I got
close look at the killer through field glasse
although he was a long way off and figured he cou
not be seen. He was a tall, thin, scarecrow *homb*

ith straw-like hair, riding a brown horse that
ad one white foreleg. That Winchester is the one
sed to kill Snark the other day, and I just took it
ıt of your saddle-scabbard, Jackson!'

Jackson cursed and levelled the Winchester at
evlone, trying to work the action. When he
ıscovered the weapon was jammed he dropped it,
nd at that moment Stanton's sixgun blasted,
ıssing a slug into the centre of Jackson's skinny
ıest. The ambusher's hard face contorted and he
ıtched sideways and crashed to the floor.
evlone faced Stanton, who was grim-faced, gun
ınoking in his hand.

'You didn't need to kill him, Art!' he rapped,
ondering if it had been done to close the man's
ıouth.

'You don't figure so, huh?' Stanton shook his
ead sadly and holstered his gun as he walked
round the desk. He rolled Jackson on to his back
nd grasped the dead man's right arm, pulling
ıck the sleeve of the jacket. 'I saw him flick his
ıgers and knew what he was going to do. Take a
ok!'

Devlone saw a quick-draw rig fastened to
ıckson's right forearm, and a .41 derringer was
ctually clutched in his dead fingers.

'You were as good as dead,' Stanton said softly,
xcept that I knew Mal Jackson pretty well and
ead his movements!'

'Thanks!' Devlone nodded slowly. 'You saving
y life killed some nasty suspicions I had in
ıind!'

Range Grab

Stanton frowned, waiting for an explanatio
but Devlone shook his head. He suddenly realiz
that he was holding his breath, and sighed to r
himself of tension. Now it really was all over b
the shouting, and there would be plenty of th
before the due processes of the law were final
carried out. But that was not a part of his dut
He holstered his gun and tried to relax, thinki
that now would be a good time to get some sleep.